MUR DERA

Destroys

HIS PHIUCHA

Mur Dera Destroys His Phiucha

JM Carydice

Carydice Books, England

Printed in the United Kingdom

First, 2018

ISBN 978-1-9996226-0-2

TABLE OF CONTENTS

PREFACE

I remember sitting at the edge of my bed wondering, what should I do? After reading an advert for a short story competition online.

I'd not too long ago published a children's book, and was looking to increase my sales. Don't get me wrong, a number of family members and friends had purchased copies of the book, and the general feedback was very promising. People said my story was intriguing and educational, which boosted my confidence immensely. But compliments weren't enough. I needed more sales.

I had produce a quality item, yet had not done a book launch or a radio interview at that stage. Neither had I made any public appearances, to assist with the promotion of the book. So my product was not getting the recognition it deserved.

For days I battled within, wondering whether I should or shouldn't.

I knew if I wanted to achieve, then I needed to proceed. So I found myself a comfortable little spot and without further delay, began to write and did not stop until I had completed a four hundred word story. It turned out to be a good little read in the end: So I was told by my critiques. I was pleasantly surprised. Many suggested it would be great as a novel, so that is precisely what I did. Instead of entering the competition, I transformed my short story into a novel.

'Mur Dera Destroys his Phiucha (Phiucha pronounced future),' is a fictional heart wrenching tale about a cheating liar and a fraud. The protagonists pays dearly for his misdoings and although he deserves the punishment he receives, one cannot help but feel pity for him as his life spirals down.

Married Mur is a womaniser who doesn't care much for anyone's feelings but his own. His life then takes an unexpected turn for the worst, and forces him to go on the run. He begins to live as a fugitive and during this period experiences much misfortune. He has to deal with situations that would madden the strongest of men and he does reach a point where he feels he cannot cope anymore.

But Mur is given a second chance, an opportunity to turn over a new leaf

Will he start afresh or does he duplicate the sins of his past? This novel deals with some strong and sensitive issues, and it has a number of thrilling twists and turns, nonetheless it is an extremely enjoyable and thought provoking read.

CHAPTER ONE

I could barely feel the tips of my fingers that icy Friday morning of January 1988. It was bitterly cold, and I was in my Ford Capri 3000E, frantically speeding south down the Motorway.

The road was dark and lonesome, and I could not help but wonder whether I had made the right decision, to leave my hometown so sudden.

Maybe it was a bit hasty of me. But at the same time, I knew I really didn't have much choice.

I was in trouble, deep trouble and had to make a quick getaway. My life was in danger, under threat, and I was being forced to flee my lovely home town, Liverpool. The upheaval was daunting. Totally demoralising.

So I was selfishly racing down the M6. Doing eighty miles an hour, when I should have been driving at seventy miles or below. Putting not only my life, but the lives of other motorists at risk, because I had messed up.

I'd done something terrible, and was now in a confused state, and through my despair I was running.

Before I had left out, I promised myself I would not ease my speed for anyone. Well, not until I was safely on the M1 - *where I believed I would mostly be out of danger*.

My situation was dire, overwhelming, and I was truly grief stricken.

The name is Mur by the way, Mur Simon Dera. But most people call me Murderer. I'm a 6ft 2in Nubian of Caribbean descent. I have an average build, an oval face, a straight nose, large almond shaped hazel brown eyes, full black lips and high cheekbones: which gives me a chiselled look and I usually wear my hair very low, but not bald.

Being named Mur with a surname like Dera was just wrong? I blame mother! She named me.

I would often ask myself *whilst growing up*, "Why did mother do that? Name her son Mur, with a surname like Dera.

My school years were hell because of it. Some days worse than others. The kids where unrepentant. At least one of them would jeer me when I entered the classroom with something like "Look out, the Mur Dera's about!" They use to get on my nerves.

I remember once, a group of boys in my class had teased me practically for the whole day. So that evening when I got home from school, *still upset and crying,* I asked mother why? W*hy did you name me Mur*? I asked. "Where did that name come from?" I just wanted to know! Mother looked me straight in the eye.

"Hush son!" She said, and hugged me whilst softly rubbing my head. "You would have died at birth if it wasn't fah that nice Dr Lampon. Dr Mur Lampon him name! The delivery doctor!" Her expression was so sincere. So sorrowful.

Mother was Jamaican. "Is him help bring you into this world. You was small an weak and the umbilical cord did tie round you neck. You nearly dead! Thank God fah doctor Lampon!"

A solitary tear had slipped down mother's cheek, as she spoke in her soft Jamaican accent. Mother always claimed she was lucky to have me. Said I was fortunate to be alive.

Nonetheless, naming me after the obstetrician wasn't in my favour. Saviour or not, she should have shown her appreciation in some other way.

I would usually stop in Birmingham and visit a friend or two, when driving down the M6. But not that morning. Things were different. I was on a mission. A journey I wholeheartedly believed I would probably never return from.

My destination was Southend, Essex country. A girlfriend of mine (Isabelle), had made arrangements for me to stay at her hut. Which was on family land far out in the sticks.

Isabelle felt I would be safe there. Well at least until all that was going on had died down. The hut was within walking distance from some woodlands (so if for any reason I needed somewhere to hide, I wouldn't have very far to go).

First however, I needed to stop off in London. At a place called Stratford. I wanted to leave my car there, to hopefully throw those seeking me completely off my track. Stratford was one of the few places south of England that I knew pretty well. Having travelled there a number of times during my teen years. My plan was to get to Stratford, park up the car, make my way to the train station, where I would catch a train from there straight to Southend. It probably wasn't the best route, but for me that way was fine.

I continued speeding down the motorway and once I was on the M1, cruised for the rest of my journey.

I was knackered by the time I hit the capital. But I didn't stop until I got to London's East End and when I arrived in Stratford, I immediately began searching for somewhere to park.

I was looking for a quiet spot, one well-hidden, so I could avoid being seen by anyone who knew me.

But finding somewhere suitable, was proving to be far more of a challenge than I had anticipated. London streets were hectic. Way busier than the streets of Liverpool. Especially for that time of the morning.

People were rushing about, doing this and doing that. The place looked so overcrowded, and it was beginning to make me feel claustrophobic. Very uncomfortable.

I had driven from one road to the next, hoping to find a parking spot soon.

It eventually took me around twenty minutes to park up. Courtesy of one dumb HGV driver. Who had taken a wrong turn and forced me onto a side street. Fortunately, the street led to a huge derelict housing estate, which gates had been left wide open!

Initially, I was apprehensive to enter and I wasn't very comfortable about leaving my car on an estate I never knew existed until that point. Nevertheless I took my time and drove in.

Upon seeing the state of the buildings. I first thought "my goodness!" Every single block looked dilapidated. Absolutely rotten! Unsightly and grim. There were loads of open garages on it. Some broken, others packed to the brim with rubbish. But I did notice there were a few that appeared to be in an okay condition. So I drove closer to check them out.

I had only bought my car a few months back, and I had purchased it from new. I loved that car. So it wasn't going to be easy leaving it behind?

"Damn!" I cursed under my breath. I really wasn't ready for this.

So many changes had taken place, in such a short space of time. Changes I would never have believed possible, had they not directly affected me.

It was all getting to my brain: having to flee Liverpool, leaving my wife and now having to abandon my vehicle, on some shitty housing estate.

Life was really pushing me around!

I didn't even want to think about travelling without my car. The only good thing about the entire scenario was the estate being situated at the back of 'Stratford Grove,' was less than a stone's throw from the train station. So I wouldn't have far to walk.

As I parked my vehicle up, I began to think about my life back home in Liverpool, before all the trouble started. It wasn't a perfect life or overly fantastic, but it was a good and pleasant life that had dramatically changed overnight.

Within the blink of an eye, my popularity had subsided. People who once loved me, were now out for my blood. I was being pursued like some wild animal, and I wasn't even sure of the cause. They were predators, very last one of them.

Had I remained in Liverpool another night, I probably would have perished. It was perplexing how rapidly things change. But I suppose in many ways I needed to be thankful that I hadn't been buried alive in a ditch somewhere!

Every second that passed was a worrying moment. Where was I going? Where would I end up? I felt like I was living a nightmare. I wasn't sure of anything anymore.

I still had a distance to travel. Which was terribly unnerving. Especially knowing that everything about my life would soon be different. It was making me jittery.

I needed to calm down, and fast, before I travelled any further.

Music often relaxed my soul. I loved my music, and I was particularly fond of Lover's Rock; a passionate style of reggae with a soft sound. I kept loads of music cassettes in the glove compartment of my car. So I reached for one and put it on to play. "Wolves and Leopards" blared out from the speakers, and by the time it got to the chorus part I was rocking from side to side and nodding my head to the beat.

The music did begin to relax me. Well kind of…
But before long I started to feel melancholic.

The song was reminding me of happier times, joyful
moments that I had spent with my wife, Phiucha. Those
were moments I sincerely believed I would never live to see
again. It was agonising listening any longer.

Quickly, I ejected the cassette from the player, and
switched the car engine off. Then I reached into my jacket
pocket and pulled out a packet of fags, and as I lit one up
my hands began to shake furiously.

I was dying for a cigarette. The last time I had
smoked was when I stopped to refuel the car by the Blue
Boar service station, at junction 15a off the M1, and that
was ages ago.

It was strange puffing a cigarette whilst being seated
in my car. That was total misconduct in my opinion. I
would never normally smoke in anyone's vehicle, as it goes.
I absolutely abhorred the smell that accompanied stale ash
and tobacco. But today was going to be an exception. I
would smoke in my car and I wouldn't give two hoots. I
told myself. I had no energy to worry or even care about
trivial matters like the odour of a cigarette in the car. I was
feeling so rotten. My soul was in its own zone, and felt as if
it were being torn from my body. I just couldn't see myself
recovering from this unrest.

Was my life dissolving? It probably was! Because
it seem to be crumbling before my very eyes, and there was
nothing I felt I could do to prevent it.

I gazed out of my car window and looked up. It was as if I was having a vision. I could see all that I had left behind. Images appearing one after the other, then disappearing just as quickly as they had appeared. Images of my house, my business, my girlfriend, my wife, my life.

I sighed and took another pull of my cigarette and began to blow smoke rings and when the cigarette was nearly half done, for some unknown reason I dabbed the rest of it out on my immaculately kept dashboard.

"Yes!" I shouted angrily - *at my car*. "I'm leaving you behind!" I could hear the frustration in my voice, and believed if anyone had been passing at that moment and had overheard me, they would swear I was some kind of nutcase. For I spoke to the car as if I were speaking to a real person.

I really wanted to bawl. But could not bring myself to do so.

Aggrieved, I raised both hands above my head.

"Why? I yelled, *with so much frustration in my voice*, before slamming them heavily down onto the steering wheel. My heart ached.

"Tell me why!" I shook and looked up to the sky.

I felt like punching something, anything. Just to release a little of the frustration I was feeling within.

"Twenty-two years we were together and now this!" I shouted. How despairing.

I was truly disappointed in myself. For I knew I only had me to blame. It was I who had caused all the problems in my life. Me and my disgusting behaviour. I

16

was a victim yes, but only of my own transgression. For I was the one who had cheated on Phiucha (not the other way round) and it was me who had instigated the altercation.

My troubles started days earlier. On the Wednesday afternoon. When I had returned home from work, early.

Instead of letting myself in through the front door, I walked around the side of the house to check the garden. As I would usually do. However what I saw almost maddened me.

I became enraged and attacked two innocent people. The man was in a pitiful state when I fled the scene. For I had really hurt him (an act I now regretted, tremendously).

Everything about my actions that afternoon was heinous, unwarranted, and looking back I just cannot fathom what had come over me. It was probably guilt.

My behaviour was that of a madman. An absolute maniac, and to add insult to injury, I did not remember a thing about it until I received a call from a friend, later that evening.

Marcus Cummings my good mate, wanted to know exactly what had taken place at the Dera's household. We were close Marcus and I. We grew up together, and had attended the same schools. So Marcus knew me inside out and vice versa.

He told me, some disturbing news was going around, and said he'd heard it from reliable source. Marcus claims he couldn't rest until he spoke with me personally. Said he actually came home early that evening just to make the call. I was at Isabelle's house when he phoned. Which was around 10pm, and when he began to talk about some of the things that were being said, I was at a loss. Dumbfounded. Completely baffled by what I was hearing. I sat on Isabelle's couch with the phone at my ear, listening in disbelief. And although the incident had only taken place a few hours before he called, I personally could not remember a thing about it.

At one point I even wondered if Marcus was making everything up. Absolutely nothing he was telling me made sense. I now realise I was in a fugue state, which had happened to me once before. Years ago.

But back then my entire memory had disappeared. But only for a few days.

Marcus ended the conversation with a warning. Told me to leave "The Pool" as soon as I could. Said there was big trouble ahead, and I should try and get out long before anyone learns of my whereabouts.

According to Marcus I was now a marked man. Some dreadful people were hunting me down, and they were planning my demise. He said talk of what they intended to do with me, was so gruesome it had sent chills down his spine. But what troubled him the most, were the threats from Dillon Collins.

Dillon was a crazy son of a bitch, a notorious gangster. And worst of all, he was also cousin to my wife, Phiucha.

Ruthless in every way, Dillon was not a good enemy to have. Marcus and I knew if Dillon was looking for you, you were more or less already caught. The man had the reputation of feeding his enemies to pigs. Although personally, I didn't know of anyone that he had actually done that to. There was a lot of hearsay going on.

Word on the street was Dillon wanted to slit my throat. I couldn't believe it. My own cousin in law wanted to slit my throat.

God bless Marcus for warning me. He knew full well he was putting his own life at risk. But said he felt somewhat compelled to inform his friend of the dangers that lay ahead. Told me it was standard, and a risk he was prepared to take.

There was no other way forward, I couldn't ignore Marcus's revelation. We both knew my only chance of survival was to leave Liverpool. Within forty eight hours maximum.

Marcus and I said our goodbyes and as soon as I replaced the receiver, I spoke with Isabelle.

The following morning Isabelle made arrangements for me to leave Liverpool. I was to go down to a hut on her family's land, and she would join me the next day. The Saturday.

Immediately I packed a light travelling bag and waited until the early hours of Friday morning, then alone, I slipped out into the dead of the night.

Still seated in my car, I turned to look at its interior. This Capri had taken me nearly twelve months to purchase, and I had to slog my guts out hard and long and save every spare penny to buy it. The amount of days and weeks I went without. Not just me, but Phiucha as well. We put many of our needs aside to get this vehicle.

I bought the car brand new, because after problems I'd had with previous motors, I promised myself I would never buy another used vehicle again. It was too much hassle replacing parts. Which wasn't worth my money or my time.

Not only that, I had customised the car with private number plates, new alloy wheels, and a top of the range Kenwood stereo system, that cost me a small fortune.

I never really had any children to call my own. Only a son that had been adopted out at birth. So I made my car my baby, and gave it a name. Shirley I called it, and wherever I went, so did Shirley.

I wanted to store every detail of Shirley in my memory. Just the thought of leaving Shirley behind, was making my situation more difficult.

I again turned my head and took one last glance at the car's interior, then I gathered my possessions and exited the vehicle, and as I walked away, I refused turn around. Just in case I became tempted to jump right back into the car and drive off.

I steadily made my way to the station, and headed straight for a ticket kiosk.

"One way to Southend!" I politely asked a short stocky man, neatly dressed in his British Rail uniform.

"That we be two poun and twenty-foive pee, tank yu very much sir!" said the cashier. The man sounded Bajan.

I handed him a crisp five-pound note, and in return he gave me my ticket and some change. The time was 9:40 but my train wasn't due to depart until 10:00, so I popped into WH Smith to pick up a few snacks, plus something I could read during my journey.

I grabbed a bag of crisps, two cans of ginger beer, a couple chocolate bars, and a magazine. Then I made my way to the checkout.

Six people were standing in the queue ahead of me, a possible seven, if the woman and her teenage looking son, intended to pay separately.

I waited patiently in line, for my turn. But the queue seemed to be at a standstill.

"That damn cashier!" I grumbled. She was young and slim. Blond headed, and probably in her early twenties. The woman seemed to be chatting away with one of the customers for a very long time. It irritated watching her. *If she continues.* I told myself. *She's going to make me miss my train!*

I decided I'd give her a little while longer, before saying something! But before I had a chance to open my mouth, the queue began to decrease, and when it was down to the last three customers, an odd-looking Caucasian couple walked into the shop. They picked up a newspaper and a packet of mints, then joined the back of the queue.

I took an instant dislike to them. From the second they stepped in line. I could feel them scrutinising me. It wasn't for long mind, but it was long enough to arouse my suspicions.

I stood sideways and began secretly watching them from the corner of my eye. They were penetrating my very being. Looking me up and down, and whispering to one another. It was annoying to say the least, and as much as I tried to ignore them, I couldn't.

Seconds later, the man mentioned something about a flying jacket. Which was really odd, because that is precisely what I was wearing. A tanned flying jacket. No other customer in the shop had a flying jacket on — only me!

I glared at the couple menacingly, to warn them not to go there. My temper was rising. Partially because I wasn't in a good place. I began to feel provoked and so hoped my analysis was wrong. I know I can be off-key at times. Especially when I feel vulnerable. I can get sort of paranoid.

But I wasn't being paranoid that day. Nor was I imagining things. As soon as the couple realised I'd stopped paying them attention, the man again spoke, but a lot louder this time. As if deliberately trying to prompt a reaction from me.

"Nelly!" he said to his female companion. "That fellow looks a lot like him, don't you think?"

The old man was kind of grubby in appearance and seemed to be of retirement age. His fingertips were stained a brownish yellow. That colour commonly associated with heavy smokers, and he was quite small in stature. The man wore his beard like Santa. Long, bushy, and white, and he was wearing baggy off coloured clothing, which made him look rather smelly.

"What was that, Barry Malory?" The woman asked. She was a dumpy little thing. Short and stout, with a large round face that bore the likeness to a pig. Flamboyantly dressed, the little woman sported ginger curls on shoulder-length hair and had on a fluffy fluorescent pink jacket, which she wore with bright purple jeans that looked at least a size too small for her.

"I was thinking the same thing" she said.

That was it. I had heard enough.

"Who?" I asked sharply.

The old couple looked at each other nervously, even though it was them that had instigated my response. They both hung their heads low and were showing signs of unease. But neither of them dared make any attempt to answer me.

"Who are you talking about?" I asked. I could see a classic situation evolving, one where the victim was going to be made to look like the perpetrator. But I wasn't backing down. "Me?" I indicated, pointing my forefinger to my chest.

I was fuming and had almost reached boiling point. Then an inner voice whispered sharply, "keep calm, Mur!"

It almost sounded like my mother speaking, so I took heed.

The couple had stirred me up though, and I was now in a terribly foul mood.

"To hell wid dem Philistines!" I cussed under my breath. "Dem nuh no who dem ah mess wid!"

I spoke in a Jamaican accent, which I often did when I was upset. What I really wanted to say however, was tell them where the hell to go. I was so relieved when the woman in front of me and her son walked up to the checkout. I was next in line.

That's when I spotted the newspaper. It was on a stand a few feet away. There was a photograph of a man on it, who looked awfully familiar. But as it was a little distant, I could not make out the face properly.

Intrigued, I stepped aside, to try and take a closer look. Simultaneously, the mother and son had finished being served, so no one in the queue had been waiting any great length of time for me to go to the checkout.

"Hurry up nuh!" shouted a scar-faced Rastafarian out of the blue. The man was at the end of the queue.

"Me in a hurry you nuh star!" He yelled. His outburst really surprised me. The guy hadn't even given me a chance.

Mystified, I held my chin between my thumb and forefinger and looked him straight in the face. "Supm nuh right!" I said aloud. I was beginning to feel under fire. First by Tweedle Dum and Tweedle Dee (the elderly couple), and now by this obnoxious natty dread.

"Weh you ah deal wid Iyah?" I asked the man.

All this drama!" I thought, and by the look on my face, I am sure the Rasta man knew if he said another wrong word, I would kick off. There was no doubt in my mind the situation could become physical. And that, I wanted to avoid.

The man rolled his eyes. "Every ting cool, boss!" He said, without even looking at me. His response was brief, but it mellowed me down as quickly as it had wind me up.

I held my head high and made my way to the counter without saying another word.

Once I paid for my goods, I walked over to the stand and picked up a copy of the newspaper.

I glanced down at the picture and read the headline, and I almost choked on the spot. Thank goodness, my back was turned to the other customers in the shop. For if anyone had seen the look of surprise upon my face, it would have widened their curiosity. People would certainly have noticed that something wasn't right.

WANTED IN CONNECTION WITH! I read. Printed in large black bold font and plastered across the top of the front page!

What is really going on? I pondered. I decided to take a sneak peek behind me, just to see if anyone had seen a change in my demeanour. My head felt like it would burst for a hot second. And I was becoming breathless.

Man and woman hospitalised after brutal attack, I further read. *Both are currently fighting for their lives.*

How was this possible? I knew I had hurt the man, but not Phiucha. I had no idea she would need to be fighting for her life.

Surely someone, somewhere had got the whole story wrong! *It's a load of bull!* I told myself.

An unexpected dizziness suddenly swept over me. My hands felt sweaty and my feet felt as heavy as rocks. I grabbed on to a shelf to stop myself from toppling to the ground. I couldn't bear to read any more.

Hmm… This was the cause of Dillon's aggression! And rightfully so. It was all coming back to me. Slowly but surely. I was remembering more!

I'm in some serious shit. I thought.

And this explains the strange behaviour from the old couple!

They must have seen the newspaper, and recognised me. News had travelled fast and I was at the forefront. Time was rapidly running out. My freedom was about to expire.

I needed to make tracks. Get myself out of the shop, and leave London before anyone else recognised me.

I had a pair of sunglasses in my pocket, so I put them on, and took a woolly hat from my bag, and fixed it so it sat above my eyes but covered both my ears and most of my forehead.

Then quietly, I slipped out of the shop completely unnoticed.

CHAPTER TWO

I checked the time on my watch. It was 9:54, which meant I didn't have long to catch my train.

"Shit, man!" I cussed. The train was due to depart in six minutes and if I didn't get a move on I was going to miss it. I began running towards the platform.

"I'm not going to make it!" I repeatedly grumbled. But luckily I caught the train in the nick of time, and had to board the second carriage *where I didn't want to be*, instead of the end carriage, where I felt I ought to be.

I wasn't too displeased however. For no one had noticed me. Neither could anybody see my full face, with the hat and glasses on. I wanted to avoid any form of eye contact, so there was no way I could remain in a carriage full of passengers. Even though I now looked completely different, to how I looked when the picture in the newspaper was taken.

With my face turned towards the window, I stood in the corridor and waited for everyone to be seated. Then swiftly, I walked down the aisle and through several carriages, without looking either side. I just kept walking, and didn't stop until I reached the carriage at the end.

The headline I just read, had shook me up. I was blown away, and all I wanted to do, was sit down and meditate.

When I arrived at the end carriage and opened the door, it was practically empty inside, and I felt relieved. There were only two people seated. One near the front and the other almost central. All the back seats were vacant, so I literally had the pick of the bunch.

I cautiously made my way to a seat and placed my bags in the overhead compartment before sitting down. I didn't want anyone asking me any questions, so I covered my face with the magazine I'd just bought and pretended to be asleep.

The train ran fast down the track, and with my head still hidden beneath the magazine, I prayed my journey would end without a single disturbance.

But approximately thirty minutes into departure, a short thin Asian inspector stood over me. "Ticket please, sir!" said the little man.

I reached in my trouser pocket for my ticket but couldn't find it. The ticket wasn't there. I began to panic and I search every part of me frantically. For a moment, I worried that I may have dropped it whilst rushing to catch the train.

"I did buy a ticket!" I said to the inspector. Trying to reassure him as well as myself, that I still had the ticket in my possession. Then I remembered, I had put the ticket straight in my bag as soon as I'd bought it. I pulled down my bag down from the overhead compartment, opened it up, took out the ticket and handed it to the inspector. He tore off his section and gave me my part, and for a second time I placed the magazine over my face, relaxed back into the chair and again pretended to be asleep.

In and out I snoozed for most of the journey, and by the time the train arrived at Victoria Station in Southend, I felt a little more energised.

I didn't want to hang around, so I headed straight to the beachfront. I was feeling so stressed and still very worried about being recognised.

Plus it just dawned on me that t*oday was officially going to be my last day of freedom, so I should try and make the most of it.*

When I got to the coast it was very windy, but the cold breeze against my face, felt somewhat refreshing. I was truly thankful I had reached safely.

Everything I valued and loved, was no more, and what I needed now was solace. Peace!

Just thinking about how things could have turned out made me shudder. My situation might have been far worse. I could have ended up in prison, or worse still, in the stomach of a pig.

I was grateful I was able to walk along the seashore that day, and as I gradually paced myself up and down, I could feel the little rock stones beneath my shoes, but I walked and walked until I was tired. Then I sat on the sea wall, and looked across the Thames Estuary. My butt was freezing cold, and getting damp. The wall was icy and the dampness had soaked through my trousers.

But I wasn't about to move. Just being in Southend made me feel better.

I first visited the place with Phiucha, back in August 1971. We came down here alone, without the consent of our parents, and we ended up staying in Southend for just under a week. Six days to be precise. Neither of our families had any idea where we were.

We just got up early one morning and I suggested to Phiucha we jump on a train and head south. There was no particular destination in mind, and we hadn't brought any spare clothes or essentials with us. All we had was money. Lots of it. Around four hundred and ninety-three pounds to be precise, and we were off.

It was a fantastic week away. We were in and out of the fairground. Racing on the beach. Go-karting, swimming, sunbathing, making love. Eating all we could manage, from the various restaurants along the promenade. I would stuff my face with cockles and shrimps practically every night, and we would smoke pot. I took speed, stole little rock sweets from the local shops (just for the fun of it). Phiucha and I did so much, and later in the day, we would sit at the edge of the long pier and feed the seagulls whilst we ate fish and chips. Almost every single evening we did this.

I had booked us into a bed and breakfast for five nights, and on our last night we stayed at the Southern Beach Hotel. An all-inclusive treat, from me to my Phiucha. It was remarkable and the best holiday I ever had to date, even though our parents had reported us missing.

Memories of my stolen week away was great, but right now was not the time for me to reminisce. Evening was about to fall, and I would soon need to make some tracks.

I wasn't really ready to go just yet, but there was no way I could hang around the coast for much longer. I probably stood out like a sore thumb. As I had not seen any other black faces since my arrival.

The one thing I did intend on doing before I left however, was to have a stiff drink, and play some Pac Man and Space Invaders in one of the arcades. So I hastily darted across the road in search of a pub.

The first pub I came across was the horse and cart, so I walked in and saw a handful of punters sipping their drinks. This included four skinheads, who were standing around a snooker table chatting to each other. The reception was cold, and within seconds of me entering the building one of the skinheads gave me such an unwelcoming glare, I told myself I certainly won't be hanging around this place for long. I didn't want to appear intimidated however, so I walked up to the bar and ordered myself half a pint of lager, which I literally downed in one.

When I was done I casually asked an old man sitting near the entrance door, for directions to the nearest off-licence and off I went.

I bought myself two cans of Special Brew, then returned to the sea front, and again leant on the damp wall, where I slowly drank my drinks.

For the rest of my time at the coast I was in and out of the arcades, until darkness had engulfed the skies. By then I was more than ready to leave. Sad to be going, yes, because I didn't know if, or when I would ever be back, and in all honesty I was even tempted to book myself into a hotel for the night. But I knew a decision like that could be disastrous and cost me dearly.

My next move was to quickly flag down a taxicab, so that is what I did.

"Middy Manor please!" I said to the cabbie and jumped in.

The cab driver was a heavy-looking bearded chap, that couldn't wait to initiate a conversation with me once I was seated.

"Where are you from?" He asked.

To which I replied "Liverpool."

"Oh you're a Scouser, then?"

"I sure am!"

Thomas Monahan, was fascinating. He spoke with a strong East End accent. Which I personally found intriguing. Every word expelled from his mouth put a smile on my face.

He was very open about his home life, and spoke of the many problems he and his wife were going through with their strong-headed, rebellious, teenage sons. They were identical twins, and causing pure mayhem: partying, boozing, and having friends stay over for most nights of the week.

As Thomas spoke it bought me back to my own childhood. With my parents. Had I ever tried that sort of crap with any of them, my ass would have got a proper whooping (especially from my mother),

My parents were strict Jamaican Christians, and my mother was a woman who wouldn't hesitate to put you in order. She kept a belt on show. Her rod of correction she called it. Which she hung on the passage wall, facing the front door. It was one of the first things you saw when you entered the house, and it was there has a constant reminder, not to bring any nonsense from the street into her home.

Both my mother and father fully endorsed physical punishment. They were great believers of that old biblical fable, if you spare the rod you spoil the child!

I said nothing to Thomas. I could barely tackle my own problems, let alone take on anyone else's.

Thomas stopped about ten yards from the east gate, which was approximately a quarter of a mile from the main road. And before I exited his cab, I paid my fare, and thanked him, then watched as he drove off into the night.

The five-bar field gate was entrance to a private road that led you straight to the manor.

It was locked, which is why Thomas could take me no further. Isabelle had told me the family always kept the east side gate locked. As nobody ever used it. This meant I had another quarter of a mile to travel on foot, before I would finally reach my destination.

No one up at the manor knew anyone would be staying by the hut, and that was the way me and Isabelle wanted it to remain. I had no intention of ever going to the main house at all.

The land surrounding the manor was quite large and it was all owned by Isabelle's grandfather. Isabelle had drawn me up a map with directions on how to get to the hut, so I knew it would not be too difficult for me to find.

I'd never been to the place before, but imagined it wouldn't be much warmer there, than where I was currently standing. It was very cold out that evening. Much colder than it had been earlier. I was freezing. Tired too.

I truly didn't know what to expect. Isabelle said the place was okay, but to her everywhere was okay. She had packed a flashlight in my bag, so I took it out and without further ado, was off with my torch and the map, to begin the long trek to the hut.

As I walked along the footpath, I began to feel really alone. The path was dark, narrow and very eerie, and after a few hundred yards, it opened out into a big field.

The field was enormous and brightly lit. But for some reason, I felt even less comfortable and more exposed walking through the field, than I had done whilst on the path. I certainly didn't want to continue using the flashlight in such a wide-open space as I believed it would draw unnecessary attention. Even though I was now far from the main road. The moon was full that evening however, and it was a better source of light. So I switched off the torch and used the moon light instead.

Walking through the field was giving me the heeby-geebies. The slightest noise or movement was startling and made me jump.

"This is crap!" I hissed. I couldn't believe the position I was in. Up until that point I don't think I'd given much thought to the real horror of my situation. It was only now that I was alone and without distraction, things were finally beginning to sink in.

The reality was despairing and sickened my stomach to the core. Marcus and Isabelle were the only two people who knew the real reasons for my sudden departure from Liverpool. No one else knew anything. None of my employees, nor family members, or friends. Just Marcus and Isabelle.

I had told Isabelle about the confrontation. And admitted to punching Phiucha once, as well as beating up the guy. However, I did not mention anything me and Marcus discussed over the phone. In terms of me being in grave danger, so poor Isabelle was under the impression that I would only be leaving town for a short while, or until things died down.

I and Marcus on the other hand knew differently. We both wondered whether I'd ever be able to return to Liverpool again.

I could not stop thinking about the newspaper article. I just couldn't get the headline out of my head. Especially the part about Phiucha. So much of what I'd forgotten, was gradually coming back to me. My memory was surely returning, and I was now wondering how the heck I had gotten myself in such a mess. What had unleashed the beast in me?

I was terribly concerned about the condition Phiucha was in. For according to the paper, her state was critical and she was fighting for her life.

But how was that possible? Phiucha didn't deserve this. None of it. *Oh, I wish I could go to the hospital and see her!* I know I didn't show it often, but truth is, Phiucha was everything to me! She was my absolute world, and now she was fighting for her life in some hospital bed alone, and I was far away from her.

CHAPTER THREE

It had taken me almost fifteen minutes to do half the journey, and I still felt as vulnerable as I had done, when I first started out.

The wind was torturously strong and slowing me down considerably. My face had begun to sting, as if I was being attacked by a swarm of bees and I could hear strange noises all around. I even thought I saw a pair of eyes staring through the overgrown grass at some point. Plus I felt hungry too. I hadn't eaten much all day, *only the few snacks I bought from the train station*, and that was ages ago.

I should have asked Thomas to stop by a shop on the way. But I don't remember even seeing any open. Oh why hadn't I come better prepared?

If I had my car things would certainly have been different. I so wish I didn't have to leave Shirley back in London. I could have parked her up on some dark road, and slept in her for the night.

Anyway I couldn't moan too much. It was all my own doing why I was in this position. None of this upheaval would ever have been necessary, had I not jumped the gun. Oh why did I ever doubt Phiucha? She'd never betrayed me before! So I really had no sound reason to question her dignity.

But I had to blame someone. It could never have been all my fault. That was the problem! It always had to be someone else's doing. Never mine. They too had to be guilty. Not just me. Yet it was often I who would commit the offence.

Poor Phiucha, I had accused that diamond of a woman wrong fully. And punished her for something she didn't do. I was the problem. The deceitful one. Not Phiucha. She wasn't disloyal! She was wholesome, genuine, and an excellent wife. Phiucha's only crime was loving me, but my crime was loving myself.

It's obvious I saw only what I wanted to see that afternoon. I realise this now. But knowing now was too late. Phiucha had already been hurt.

I leaned my head back and looked up to the heavens. "Forgive me Lord!" I asked, before throwing myself to the ground. "Turn back time by twenty four!" I pleaded.

I was in a desperate state, and in need of mercy. It was pitiful. Heart wrenching. And I actually felt sorry for myself.

Big bad Mur. The fearless lion, now reduced to a pussy cat. Tears filled my eyes, but the alpha within refuse to let a single drop fall.

The moon was glistening brightly, and I watched the stars as they shimmered in the background. It was the first time I actually noticed the constellation. The true order of the stars, and how they assisted the moon in lightening the earth at night.

"Remove your wrath from me, oh Lord!" I was down on bended knees. "Let me relive the moment!" I begged "Please… Let me relive the moment!"

The ground was partially frosted, and had moistened my trouser knees. But I stayed put and began to pray. Why hadn't I listened to Phiucha when she was telling me about the surprise guest we had coming the Wednesday afternoon?

"Mur!" She'd said joyfully. I had just walked into the house to drop off the shop's daily takings. "You'll never guess what?" Phiucha sounded excited. There was so much love exuding from her that day. "We have a visitor coming tomorrow! And…"

"Hold that thought!" I interrupted as usual. "Don't ruin the surprise!"

I would often act uninterested when I didn't want to hear her out. I don't know why I behaved like that with Phiucha. I only know that I took her for granted most of the time. Yet I was happy to entertain my chicks on the side. My concubines. My other women. I was always willing to please them, but would never put myself out for my wife.

Phiucha and I hadn't seen or spoken to one another all day. Yet I couldn't even be bothered to give her a few minutes of my time.

I rarely showed interest in anything she had to say or do, and on that particular afternoon I was more concerned with meeting Isabelle, than listening to what my wife had to say. Isabelle and I had a dinner date booked for a curry, and I was already ten minutes late. For a damn curry!

"We'll talk when I get back," I promised her. "I'll only be gone a couple of hours." Those were my last words to Phiucha before I kissed her on the lips and rushed out the door.

But Phiucha knew better. She knew I wouldn't come home that night and called me a liar as I rushed to my car. "You won't be gone for a couple of hours!" She shouted. "You lying bastard!" Phuicha stood waving derisively from the threshold.

She was right. I didn't come home within the two hours, like I'd promised. Phiucha never actually saw me again, until the Wednesday afternoon.

I had spent the night at Isabelle's. A woman I had been dating for over eighteen months. Isabelle had recently told me she was sixteen weeks pregnant with our child. Me... Finally going to be a father. I was having a child.

Isabelle was a lovely woman. Generous, caring and besotted with me. And I... Well... I was very fond of her! She knew Phiucha and I were married. But was happy to remain in a relationship with me, nonetheless. From the very beginning Isabelle had stressed, she'd rather have a piece of me, than none of me at all.

It was Isabelle who advised me to stay at the hut, which was really a log cabin, she had inherited from her grandfather.

I on the other hand didn't really relish the idea of staying in the hut, nonetheless I was grateful. As I felt I was in no position to be choosey. Two fates stood before me. I

40

could either end up losing my life, or being incarcerated somewhere, and I wanted neither to happen.

With my present frame of mind, given the choice, I would be happier to welcome death, than have my liberty taken from me.

The night before last when Marcus called Isabelle's and gave me the heads up, I really didn't know whether to take him serious or not.

"Yu best git out ah de pool fast!   " Marcus had warned. "Dem bwoy ah hunt yu down like wild dawg."

Unlike me, Marcus was born in Jamaica but came to England at the age of six. One year before he was due to start junior school.

"Marcus, ah weh me do dem? I asked.

"Ah yu fi tell me dawg!" He said. "But it musee supm real bad."

Marcus spoke with conviction, and that was our last conversation. Everything was clear in my head now.

I remained on my knees deep in thought and began to visualise the attack. It was awful and I knew there was no more hiding from the truth. I could see things clearly. How badly I beat the young man, and how horrified he looked as he was held his head, trying to prevent the blood from running down the sides of his face. A small red pool had formed beneath his knees as he pulled at my shirt and pleaded for his life.

That was when I fled the scene.

As the vision of the attack slowly faded, I knew there and then I would have to pay dearly for what I had done. If not with my life, it was most certainly going to cost me my sanity.

I got up from the ground and again began making my way towards the hut.

Tears were finally trickling down my face, where I could barely see the dark structure ahead. I didn't have far to go before I would reach the small wooden building.

But my legs were aching like hell, and my shoulders were burning from the weight of the straps on my travel bag.

But I kept going and did not stop until I was finally outside the hut door.

CHAPTER FOUR

The key for the hut was under the mat, precisely where Isabelle had said. So I let myself in and switched on the light.

Yes! I thought, when I saw the sealed whiskey bottle on the table.

I was so looking forward to a drink. I had heard Isabelle ask one of the workers on the phone to clean up the hut and leave a full bottle of whiskey on the table for her. So I knew it was going to be there.

Almost straightaway I opened it up and took a couple of swigs. Then I began to observe the building.

The hut was basically one massive room, similar to a bedsit in design, but it had three doors. The front door, the back door and a side door. The side door, which was to the left of the front door, was an obvious extension of the structure, probably added much later than when the place was originally built. This door led to a bathroom. And the back directly faced the front door.

The place was furnished but looked very outdated, and although you could see it was kept fairly tidy, it also had a musty smell.

In the right-hand corner of the room was a small open-plan kitchen, with a sink that probably hadn't been used for decades, and above the sink was a dusty window with panes that resembled frosted glass. Beneath the sink were some nineteenth-century-looking floor cupboards, which could have done with a coat paint, and there were a number of garden tools randomly stacked against the kitchen wall. To the left of the room was a wooden bed, with an ultra-thin mattress and upon the mattress was a blue cotton sheet. At the foot of the bed was an ottoman-style storage box, which I opened up. In the box I found a thick blanket, a patchwork quilt, and some ugly floral bed linen, all sealed in their original wrappers!

Awkwardly placed in the middle of the room, was a slim two-seater settee and beneath the settee was a large floral rug, with an old paraffin heater upon it. I Thanked God. It was so cold.

The hut was equipped with a table and two chairs, an oil lamp, a kettle, some cutlery, a portable double gas burner, and a picnic basket. I looked in the basket and saw a loaf of bread wrapped in greaseproof paper, and a tin of carnation milk, some cheese, butter, teabags, sugar, and a can each of sardines, Spam, and corned beef. I couldn't believe my luck. I hadn't expected any food to be there and I was so hungry.

Before I did anything else, I opened up the can of sardines, broke off a piece of bread and sat at the table, and ate.

I was struggling to keep my eyes open whilst eating, and even to get up off the chair was kind of difficult. I felt overexerted. My feet were sore and swollen, from all the walking I had done. Plus my head was throbbing like crazy. I could tell someone had been in the hut that day, trying to clean up. Because alongside the musty odour, was a faint smell of disinfectant.

Eager for some sleep, I opened up some of the bedding that was in the ottoman style storage box and made myself a fresh bed. Then I removed my shoes and laid down, and within minutes of my head touching the pillow, I was out like a baby.

That night I slept right through without stirring. I didn't wake until late the next morning. Which was because I had heard some scratching noises inside the hut, and although I was still feeling tired, I quickly jumped out of bed to see where in the hut the noise was coming from. I moved stuff from one part of the room to the next, but found nothing.

After say fifteen minutes or so, I felt tired and wanted to give up, but when I went back and sat down on the bed, one of the garden tools dropped to the floor. So I slowly got up and quietly crept over to where the tools stood. It was a thin rake that had fallen, and as I looked down at the rake, I didn't take much notice of the grey furry ball type thing that was motionless behind a spade. Then its pink hairless tail moved. It was a large ugly grey rat.

Quickly I grabbed up the spade and whacked after it, but I missed. The creature swiftly darted off. I however wasn't giving up and whacked after it, and again.

The rodent began to zoom frantically across the floor, but I was determined to catch it. For I had no intentions of sharing this small hut with any species possessing more than two legs. I chased after the rat until I had eventually cornered it.

Then with one last hard smack 'Blap!' I instantly terminated its life!

At close proximately, the dead rat looked vile. I had flattened the creature, and its innards had begun to seep through its orifices. It was a ghastly sight, and made the carcass appear as if it were covered in excrement. There were small patches of blood-filled fur stuck to the back of the spade, so I ripped off some of the greaseproof paper that was wrapped around the bread, and used it to pick up the rat by its tail. I then slung the creature out the front door and washed myself down before climbing back into bed.

Tossing and turning non-stop, no matter how much I tried, I just could not get back to sleep. I had become so restless and was extremely uncomfortable. The mattress felt prickly, which I hadn't noticed earlier, and it was making me itch profusely.

I got up and pulled back the sheet to see sharp pieces of metal sticking out of the mattress, and it was those metal pieces that were digging into my flesh with every move I made.

Upon checking my skin. I could see I had been bitten all over. By either gnats or bedbugs.

There also seem to be a distinct smell of rotting grass and animal pee in the room. Which again I had not noticed before. It was gross, overpowering and had begun to make my stomach retch.

"I'm going to die!" I groaned and ran to the sink to be sick. Sweat poured from my head, as if I were in the Sahara, and my gut felt like it was going to burst. My mouth tasted raw and my whole body shivered as I vomited violently.

By the time I was done, my stomach was all pained up.

I began to reminisce on Phiucha. "She usually took care of me when I fell ill!"

"Why didn't I just walk up to them and asked who was who?"

I could envisage Phiucha lying still on a patch of wet grass in the garden.

"Damn!" I sighed. "Rude boy had don't it this time. Mur the extremist! The fanatic went the extra mile! Big ass fool! That's what he really was! A blasted fool! A desperado! Proper ediat!

And now I have to live in hiding. How Pitiful and sad!"

When I got home early from work the Wednesday afternoon, and saw Phiucha out back in the arms of another man (albeit I had spent the night at Isabelle's). I instantly lost my cool and went into a rage.

I could have walked away. But instead I chose to watch them from a distance, and as I saw this strange man holding my wife. Not knowing who he was, or why he was even at my house, I felt completely violated, and couldn't bear it, so I viciously attacked…

Phiucha had always been my number one, my only true love. She had never done me any wrong! Ever! And she was the sweetest, selfless person I knew. Phiucha had spent her life seeing to my needs, even though I didn't always deserve it. But over the last five or so years I had cheated on her over and over again. At first it was supposed to be a one off fun thing, to try someone new, because our relationship was becoming monotonous. But it went from one to two to three to four until I eventually lost count.

I would often lie to Phiucha, because of my cheating. It broke her confidence, her heart, and her trust. Time and time again, and not once did she turn her back on me!

Phiucha knew I had a dark side, but she would never make it a problem. *We had goals to achieve.* She'd say. Plans we had made together. But as with most cheats, nobody's future is ever secure. Not the cheat, their spouse, or the third person.

In a heated moment, all had been lost. I had forgotten who the real Phiucha was. How silly, to think Phiucha would stoop to my level and do to me as I had done to her.

It had only taken me a few seconds to determine her guilt. This was my flaw. Once I was consumed with wrath, there was no stopping me. I mercilessly advanced on my unsuspecting victims and inflicted blow after blow after blow.

CHAPTER FIVE

Three Days Earlier.

Phiucha Miriam Dera was on the telephone with her agent, Mark Childs. "Oh, thanks, Mark. For everything! Wish me luck!" She said before replacing the receiver.

Mark Childs was a people-tracing expert, who ran his own agency from a small office in Liverpool's city centre. He happened to be one of the best in the business and had offered to take on Phiucha's case personally. Phiucha had been looking for her son for more than ten years, and had not been successful in finding him. But within six months of Mark taking on the case he had successfully located Michael Leon Dera.

Phiucha hadn't seen Michael since she gave birth to him, which was over twenty years ago, and although she had spent more than a decade trying to trace him, not a single sighting of him had ever occurred. Nobody had any idea where Michael was. All Phiucha knew was that his adoptive family had immigrated when the lad was around five years of age. But where they went, no one could say. Phiucha wasn't even sure if her son was alive or not.

Then she registered with the MCLPA, the Mark Childs Lost People Agency, who located her son almost four thousand miles away on the Island of Jamaica. Michael's family had changed his name to Paul William

Thompson, hence the reason there was so much difficulty finding him. Phiucha couldn't get her head around the name change and would still mistakenly call him Michael, when they talked on the phone.

Fair play to Norman and Beatrice Thompson, however. Paul's adoptive parents. They never once spoke ill of Phiucha or the Lewis family. They had told Paul from a young age that he was adopted, and that his birth mother was unable to keep him due to circumstances beyond her control.

Since Phiucha and Paul had started speaking, they had truly bonded. They had a wonderful relationship, where not a week would pass without one contacting the other. Paul told his mother he never once felt unwanted by her.

And his mother explained in depth, how difficult her situation was at the time. She was just thirteen when she got pregnant with him, and fourteen when she gave birth.

Back in the day, to have a child out of wedlock was totally against her mother's beliefs.

So Phiucha's pregnancy hadn't been easy. Maybe if her mother had shown a little more compassion, things would have been better. But hard hearted Maureen Lewis condemned her daughter and made Phiucha feel disgusted with herself.

Maureen was a tough cookie to crumble and had constantly reminded Phiucha, how much she had embarrassed the family, being underage, unmarried and pregnant. It was totally unacceptable. Particularly in a Catholic household and it was considered a disgrace.

Phiucha would feel moments of anger towards her mother; she thought Maureen was the biggest hypocrite going, considering Maureen had defied her own parent's wishes and married a black man, Phiucha's father.

Phiucha dreaded the day her child would be taken from her. She couldn't bear the thought of handing her baby over to strangers. But that was her mother's orders, and it was non-negotiable.

"You'll put that child in care if you know what's good for you lass!" She'd said. "Or you'll be out on the streets and disowned by your entire family!" This was Maureen's ultimatum.

She knew tongues would wag. They had done it to her for marrying a black man; both family and friends alike. And when Phiucha's father ran off with a younger woman and left Maureen to raise their five children alone, everyone had something to say. Phiucha was the eldest of Maureen's brood, and with all the stress going on in Maureen's life, she felt there was no way she could deal with any more embarrassment. Things wasn't pleasant for her marrying outside of her race. She experienced a lot of prejudice and condemnation from many people. Maureen did not want the same happening to her daughter, regardless…

This determined her decision to send Phiucha to London, until she had her baby. Maureen made all the necessary arrangements for the child to be placed into care, as soon as it was born, and that allowed Phiucha's pregnancy to remain a secret affair. A private matter, amongst family members only.

Life was tough for Phiucha. Her father wasn't around. She hadn't seen or heard from him for at least three years prior to her pregnancy. He had a new woman and had left no forwarding address. It was only five months after Phiucha had given Michael up, that Curtis Lewis, her father, finally returned to the family home and Curtis went absolutely crazy when he learned that his daughter had a child, which had been adopted out.

Curtis wanted to try and get the child back, but it was too late; papers had already been signed. There was nothing anyone could do to alter or reverse the decision.

Phiucha had pleaded with Maureen, begging her mother to reconsider. But Maureen was unrepentant. Determined to stick to her plan. So she ignored her daughter's pleas.

As soon as Phiucha's belly started to show, she was shipped down to London to stay with her Aunt Julie. Aunt Julie was Maureen's sister. She was great to Phiucha and would spoil Phiucha rotten. However, Julie couldn't compensate for being away from her mother, and not having Maureen close by took its toll. Phiucha felt rejected and became depressed.

She would cry at night and pray for God to soften her mother's heart. But Maureen wouldn't budge. Phiucha had to remain in London until the child was born.

One measly hour is all she was allowed to spend with her son, before they took him away. During that time Phiucha held baby Michael close to her and whispered words of love in his ear. She cried and kissed him constantly, all over his tiny face.

Baby Michael was beautiful, the cutest and dinkiest baby she'd ever seen. He had piercingly blue eyes, straight black hair, and a delicate caramel complexion. All his digits were intact, and he was healthy. *Perfect*, Phiucha thought. "My son is perfect!"

But her happiness was soon to be shattered. The agony when that tall, slim brunette nurse came into the ward and took Michael away! It was traumatising. Her bump was gone, and now her baby was gone too. Phiucha cried — all that pain for nothing. Maureen had stayed with her daughter during the final weeks of her pregnancy, and was present at the birth.

Phiucha recalled looking at her mother sitting in the chair just before the nurse came and took the baby away. Maureen didn't say a single kind word to her.

"Get yourself together girl!" She had snapped, minutes after the nurse closed the door behind her.

Phiucha just had her baby taken away, and all her mother could say was "get yourself together girl." It was tough. Phiucha was inconsolable and cried her heart out. It was the first time in her life that she felt contempt towards her mother. Phiucha couldn't understand how a grandparent could permit the removal of her grandchild from its kin.

Over the years, this caused great resentment between mother and daughter. Phiucha's dislike of Maureen grew and put a wedge between them. Only when Michael turned fifteen did Maureen finally admit the truth about the night

Phiucha gave birth and why she remained so cold. She claimed it was all a front, and that she was really heartbroken over the decision she felt she was forced to make.

Arranging the adoption was the worst part, but at the time Maureen was convinced she was doing the right thing. She said when the nurse walked into the ward to take the baby away, she knew she had made the biggest mistake of her life. But she did not want to show Phiucha the slightest bit of weakness, or it would have completely broken them both, and she needed to remain strong for her daughter. Maureen knew Phiucha wanted to keep her baby but felt compelled to discourage her fourteen-year-old from welcoming motherhood so early in life. She didn't believe Phiucha or Mur were ready for parenthood and would play no role in encouraging them.

Occasionally Maureen would ask Phiucha about Michael, but this caused problems.

"Your son must be at school now!" Maureen had said round the dinner table one evening, during a family meal. It was the tenth of November, nineteen seventy three. Two days before Michael's fifth birthday. "He'll be five on the twelfth! Isn't that so Phiucha?"

Just hearing her mother mention her son's name infuriated Phiucha. *You wicked woman!* Phiucha had grumbled under her breath. Her blood was boiling.

"I can't believe you've just asked about my child in front of everyone!" Phiucha looked at Maureen and said. "Yes, Mother MY CHILD will be five years old on the twelfth of November!" Then she began to cry. "The child you forced me to give up!"

"Mo, nuh handle mi daughter suh!" Curtis quickly interceded. (Curtis called Maureen Mo for short)

The outburst led to a big argument between Phiucha and her mother. The two of them almost came to blows.

"If you wanted to know about Michael, you should never have made me put him in care?" Phiucha shouted and got up from the dinner table, before leaving the room.

Michael was her only child. She couldn't have any more children (naturally). She was told that in 1972. One year before she and her mother had that terrible argument around the dinner table. It was just after her nineteenth birthday. Phiucha was ten weeks pregnant, and bleeding heavily. She was admitted into hospital with excruciating abdominal pains.

"The baby's stuck in your fallopian tube and needs to be removed," warned the gynaecologist. It was Phiucha's last remaining tube, but her second ectopic pregnancy, since having Michael.

After surgery, she was told she would never conceive naturally again. It was devastating news and she partly blamed her mother for not having any children. But that was back then, Phiucha was a different person now. A grown woman who no longer felt any bitterness towards anyone. Especially not the woman that gave birth to her.

The last ten years of her life was spent looking for her son. She would pray most days and nights that they would one day be together. It seemed to be taking ages, but her prayers were finally answered with the assistance of Mark Childs.

Paul was delighted when Mark telephoned and said his biological mother was searching for him, for although Paul loved his adoptive parents deeply, he still wanted to know his biological family.

From when he was a young lad, he had conjured up images of how he thought his parents would look. Particularly his father, who he was dying to meet. Paul was eager to see if there were similarities between them.

Mother and son hadn't met in person yet, but time was drawing near, and neither could wait to see the other.

Paul was on a two-week vacation from the family business his adoptive parents ran. It was a successful citrus company in Jamaica, and Paul was one of the supervisors. He had taken a short break to visit Phiucha, which was scheduled for Wednesday at 1pm. He was coming to Phiucha's home, but Mur knew nothing of the arrangement. Phiucha wanted to surprise him.

That Tuesday Mur came home about an hour after Phiucha had finished speaking with Mark Childs. She was excited and wanted to tell him about their guest coming on Wednesday.

"Hi love!" She said when Mur walked in the house. He had the shop's takings with him and had come home to drop them off.

Mur rushed up the stairs to their bedroom and shortly afterwards was back down and out the door again. He hardly gave Phiucha a glance, not knowing that she had finally got in touch with their son, who was coming to visit them the following day.

He had never really forgiven Phiucha or her parents for putting his child in care without him having his say. Phiucha didn't tell him it was her mother's plan, because she knew he wouldn't have taken it well.

Phiucha wasn't too healthy now, but Mur knew nothing about her illness. Her condition was terminal and she was rapidly running out of time. She had received the news a few weeks back, shortly after she'd made contact with Michael.

Her symptoms started with the occasional headache, which was mild to begin with. Then it gradually worsened both in frequency and severity. Her vision would get blurry, but that came and went, and at times she would black out.

After the hospital ran a number of tests, Phiucha was diagnosed with an inoperable brain tumour. She hadn't told Mur or her mother about it. Being a very private person. She didn't want anyone making a fuss. Phiucha rarely shared her personal business, particularly with Mur, because he would always throw things in her face at a later date.

Mur was impatient with her, and she couldn't stand it. He had been treating her so bad of late that she was convinced he no longer wanted to be with her. Hence her decision to hide from him that she was dying. Phiucha believed his response would be far from genuine, and she didn't want any fake sympathy.

There was no doubt in her mind that he had loved her once, but not anymore. She still loved him deeply however, but Mur had stopped showing interest in her long ago. He'd become selfish, and whatever loyalty was there before, had now diminished. Communication between them was infrequent. Things were pretty bad.

So much so that Phiucha believed they shouldn't even be together anymore.

She planned to inform Mur of her condition someday. But not for now. She would put it in writing and would only be telling him what she felt he needed to know. Which would more than likely take place when she was on her deathbed. For if there was one thing Phiucha didn't want, it was Mur's sympathy, his pity during her final days, when he had mistreated her for so long.

Phiucha was always the strength in their relationship and the brains behind Mur's success. She pushed and encouraged him to pursue his dreams, whilst taking a back seat in doing anything for herself. And as soon as the business started to take off, Mur dashed her aside like an unwanted garment.

It was Phiucha who had drawn up the business plans and invested the majority of cash. All her hard-earned wages from her job as a bank clerk. Plus she had taken out a start-up bank loan, and lived below her means to build a foundation, yet she got awarded nothing. Mur was the one who reaped all the benefits and credit.

Mur kissed Phiucha on the forehead then left, promising he wouldn't be long. But Phiucha knew he was lying. She knew her husband would not be home that night. He never did come home on a Tuesday, and she had absolutely no reason to believe this week would be any different.

She watched from the threshold as Mur jumped into his car and sped off. Disappointed that he couldn't be bothered to take a short moment to hear her out, Phiucha stepped back into the house and closed the door behind her.

The rest of that evening was spent cleaning up. Phiucha wanted the place spick and span for Paul's visit.

Before she retired to bed that night, she took a nice long bath.

But no matter how much she tried, Phiucha struggled to sleep. This was a common thing when Mur wasn't home. She just couldn't rest properly without him in the house. She hated being alone at night.

It was around 3:00 that she eventually nodded off, and by 7:00 she was wide awake again. Far earlier than she intended, but up anyway.

Mur hadn't come either, which wasn't surprising. Phiucha really didn't expect him back anytime soon.

The Dera's were a hard working couple who ran their own business. A small electrical shop selling new and used goods, but specialising in television repairs. Sales weren't booming as such, but the couple were doing okay. Mur managed the shop front and Phiucha did the books from home.

All Phiucha could think of that morning was Paul. Twenty years she had waited for this day to come, and finally it was here. Phiucha felt great. Really and truly nice knowing she was at last going to be reunited with her son.

I hope I don't act foolish when he arrives, she thought to herself and walked over to her wardrobe to sort out something to wear.

It wasn't warm, so she took out a brown woollen polo neck dress, a diamante necklace, and large, hooped gold earrings.

Butterflies cascaded around in her stomach. She felt jittery and had to head for the kitchen to get herself a drink of water.

Phiucha's mother was white Irish and her father was black Jamaican, but Phiucha was English-born. Her hair was long thick wavy and brown, which she often wore back in a ponytail, and she was five foot six inches tall. Slim, but very curvy. She had full emerald eyes, a button nose and heart-shaped lips.

Quickly, Phiucha took a shower then went back downstairs to put a leg of lamb in the oven that she had marinated before going to her bed the previous night. Then she returned to her room, and began getting herself ready.

The doorbell rang dead on 1pm, so she double checked herself in the mirror before she answered it. Phiucha was nervous.

"Hello, Michael!" She greeted. Then apologised and corrected herself. "Sorry, I meant to say Paul not Michael! Hi, Paul!"

"Good afternoon, Mother!" Paul replied, and politely stretched out his arms to give Phiucha a hug and a kiss on the cheek.

Paul was stunning in person, and Phiucha glowed with pride. Her son was tall and handsome, and close enough for her to at last touch. He had a neat inch-high afro and a goatee-style beard, a pencil-thin moustache, brown hazel eyes, and a caramel colour complexion. Although he looked a little darker than when he was born. Paul was about six foot two in height and his appearance had Phiucha literally gobsmacked. He was dressed in a padded leather jacket, which he wore over a matching two-piece denim waistcoat and jeans. He looked fabulous, as far as Phiucha was concerned. She was amazed by how much he resembled his father.

Phiucha had expected her son to be handsome, for she and Mur weren't too bad-looking themselves. But nothing had prepared her for this Adonis that stood before her. She couldn't wait for Mur to come home, and see his handsome son.

"Oh, Paul!" She said and hugged him again. "Finally I get to see you in person!"

Phiucha then placed her palms upon Paul's cheeks and planted a lingering kiss on his forehead.

Tears rolled down her face. She hadn't wanted to cry in his presence, but could not stop herself. Seeing her son all grown after so long had struck a nerve, but that wasn't the only reason for her tears.

She was happy he was visiting, ecstatic, yet at the same time terribly sad as well. Her recent diagnosis was her major cause for concern. Phiucha was dying, but not ready to leave the earth as yet. She was only thirty-four.

Her eyes had blackened from the mascara she was wearing, and had left a trail of streaks down the side of her face. Without uttering a word, Paul gently pulled a handkerchief from his pocket and wiped his mother's cheeks.

They learnt so much about each other that afternoon, as they sat in the dining room talking and eating. Paul enjoyed his lunch of minted roast lamb, mash potatoes, cabbage, and peas, and after they ate they started looking through some old photographs. Paul was equally astonished at the likeness between him and his father. Phiucha let Paul know that she never once gave up hope of finding him, and that his adoption had saddened her.

Paul listened to his mother pour out her heart and assured Phiucha that she'd done him no wrong. He seemed to understand her dilemma.

His own experiences had been quite different to hers, for his childhood was a happy one. Paul's adoptive parents had raised him in a pleasant home and showered him with love. He expressed nothing but gratitude for them and thanked Phiucha for giving him life. He let her know he was blessed to have been placed with the Thompsons, and would not have wanted things to have gone any other way.

Phiucha went into the kitchen to straighten up whilst Paul continued looking at the pictures, and when she was done, she took him out the back to show off her large greenhouse, in which she grew a variety of vegetables, fruits, and herbs.

Mur had taught her much of what she knew; he was very green-fingered because he had been doing gardening since he was young.

The day was going so well. Phiucha was in her element and didn't want her time with Paul to end. She hadn't felt that good or happy in many years and was so pleased she hadn't made a fool of herself.

But as she and Paul were making their way back to the house an unexpected dizziness struck her. Paul had to hold on to his mother to steady her on her feet. Once she was sturdy, he carefully placed her arms around his neck and the two of them stood in the garden embraced.

They remained in that position for a few minutes, but Phiucha couldn't remember much afterwards, other than the thud to her head.

Before she knew it, she was waking up in a hospital bed, surrounded by physicians. They spoke openly about the young man who was found not too far from where she lay in the back garden. It was touch-and-go with him, they said. He was currently in intensive care, fighting for his life. Phiucha's eyes were closed, but she could hear them clearly. She instantly knew they were talking about her son. Paul … she could feel it in her gut.

"No!" Phiucha screamed at the top of her voice. "Not my son! Not my boy! Where is he? Where is my Paul? Call him now!" she bawled.

Her head was hurting terribly. "Ouch!" She cried and placed her hands across her forehead. She was in tremendous pain. The doctors tried to keep her calm to administer another dose of morphine.

"Relax, Mrs Dera!" said the physician who was holding her wrist. "You are in safe hands! Your son told us everything!"

But what the doctor hadn't told Phiucha was that Paul slipped into a coma shortly after he'd spoken to them.

CHAPTER SIX

It was just after eleven when I got up and went outdoors. I needed fresh air. I was so itchy, and the smell of the shack was still making me nauseous.

Isabelle was due to arrive between five and six, so I decided to check out my surroundings in the meantime.

I'd seen some woodlands less than ten minutes away, whilst I was in the cab. So I wanted to go there first. Just to see if that was the forest Isabelle had told me about.

I put on a grey hooded jogging suit, and a pair of black and white trainers, with my flying jacket. Then I left out.

As I strolled across the meadow, I kept a watchful eye. The area was deserted and I had totally underestimated the length of time it would take me to get from the hut to the woods. I had thought it would take less than fifteen minutes … But it took closer to half an hour, and as I reached the trees, I saw fungi growing wild, so I picked about a dozen, and placed them in my pocket. I loved mushrooms, and foraging. The deeper I walked into the forest, the more edibles I saw growing wild. There was dandelion, rosehip, and parsley, and although I had not come out with the intention to forage, I couldn't resist gathering stuff. I knew some of the plants well, for Phiucha and I grew a lot of foods in our greenhouse back home.

Isabelle's family's land was huge, and I was loving it. I had glimpsed a couple of deer's in the forest, and I saw a pack of foxes.

There was so much to do and to see that the time passed quickly. I must have been in the woods for a good hour or so, and I enjoyed every second I spent there. Foraging had taken me right back, to when I was a lad visiting Jamaica.

My grandfather would regularly take me on trips to his ground, and together we would dig up yams, sweet potatoes, and coco (dasheen), amongst other rooted vegetables.

If I could, I would have stayed in the woods much longer. But Isabelle was due down in a few hours, so I started making my way back.

Man… I was almost knocked out, when I opened up the hut door and let myself in. The scent of the disinfectant had virtually disappeared, and in its place was a strong, mouldy stench.

"There's no way I can sit in this" I thought, and put the things I'd gathered from the forest on the table, before going to the bathroom to get the mop and bucket.

I filled the bucket with water from the bath and added detergent and bleach, which I had found in the kitchen cupboard.

Then I made a similar solution in a bowl, and wiped down the surfaces and the rest of the furniture, as good as I could before I mopped the floor.

Time seem to pass slowly alone in the hut. The wait for Isabelle felt long. I was beginning to tire again, so I laid down on the bed and fell asleep for a short while. It was minutes to five when I heard a vehicle approaching. The car pulled up right in front of the kitchen window, and as I wasn't too sure whether it was Isabelle or not, I dived to the floor.

The engine ran for a little, then it stopped, and after that I heard the car door open and slam shut. Someone then walked up the steps and began tapping the window.

"Is anyone in there?" The person shouted. It was Isabelle. Quickly I jumped up and opened the door. Neither of us said a word. We just hugged and kissed and held one another tightly. Isabelle looked really pleased to see me, and I was so glad she was finally here. Although I felt a bit hungry and a little distressed.

"Did you bring anything to eat?" I asked.

"Of course I did!" Isabelle answered. "It's in the car." She said before going to get the shopping bags. Isabelle rustled us up some kippers, scrambled eggs, and toast, and after we ate. I began to show her the items I had gathered earlier that day. "Look what I found down by the woods!" I said pointing in the direction of the woodlands. I was standing near the window.

"Our farm is not too far from here either," Isabelle explained.

I'd forgotten all about the farm. Isabelle had told me of it ages ago; that her family's farm produced a variety of crops and reared their own livestock. We made plans to go there the following day.

The rest of our evening was spent unpacking, and when we were done Isabelle gave the place a thorough cleaning.

She seemed a little uneasy, but wasn't saying what was bothering her. I had noticed a change in her demeanour, so I asked "What was wrong?"

"I have something to tell you!" She said gently "but we'll talk later!" I left it at that, and said no more. Although I was tempted to question her further.

We were both still worn from all the travelling we'd done, so we went to bed early that night. It was an uncomfortable night. We were tossing and turning throughout, and kept waking briefly from our slumber, because our bodies were itching.

In the morning, Isabelle went up to the main house to look for a spare mattress. She, like myself, was covered in gnat bites all over her arms and legs.

*

Middy Manor was a grand luxurious fifteen-bed purpose-built property, designed by Isabelle's grandfather, Lucas Parkes himself. Lucas had inherited fifteen hundred acres of land, plus five hundred thousand pounds cash from his parents, back in the 1920's. So he built himself a dream mansion with a surround of fifteen acres.

Situated on the south side of the estate, the manor was a colossal building.

When you entered the mansion grounds via the main gate, there was a paved drive in with oak trees lined up on both sides, and surrounding the actual mansion was a long wide pebbled road, which could easily host forty plus cars.

Made from solid concrete and emblazoned on the mansion portico was the name Middy Manor, and when you walked into the building through the front door you were immediately in the lobby, which led straight to the main hall. The hall was a rectangular shape, and it had large navy blue and white squared ceramic floor tiles. Against three of the walls in the hall was small round tables, each with a large ornament on them, and a themed wall with oil paintings of various family members. In the centre of the room, hanging from the ceiling was a mammoth crystal chandelier and orderly spaced around the hall was a cream leather three-seater settee, and a pair of club chesterfield two seater suites, woven from the finest wool and satin materials.

At the back of the hall, centred, stood a stairway, and to its left was a drawing room, and to its right was a study. This was where Isabelle's grandmother usually hung out. So Isabelle made her way there first!

Lucille Parkes was sitting at her desk, looking out the window, when Isabelle walked in…

"Hi, Grandmamma!" She said sporting a big smile.

"Where have you been girl? Lucille immediately complained. We haven't seen you in ages!"

"Oh, don't say that, Nana!" Isabelle replied, as she walked up to Lucille and hugged her. "You know I love you guys!"

"Do you really?" Answered Lucille Deloris Parkes, sarcastically. She was looking rather frail since Isabelle had seen her last. "You still dating that coloured bloke?" Lucille asked.

"Hush, Grandmamma!" Whispered Isabelle, and rushed to shut the study door before anyone could hear what her grandmother was saying.

Isabelle didn't want anyone knowing about Mur just yet, and Grandmother Lucille was no good at whispering.

"Mother might hear you!" Isabelle said, and planted a kiss on Lucille's forehead. "Nana you know what Mother's like!" Isabelle's mother had never been partial to black folk.

"And don't forget, my boyfriend is meant to be our little secret!!" Isabelle added then picked up a feathered duster from the desk, and began dusting down the bookcase.

"What are you doing, child?" Asked Lucille. She knew something was up, because her granddaughter never cleaned randomly unless asked.

"I am with child!" Isabelle blurted out. "Grandmamma, I'm having a baby and I'm keeping it! I'm four months, and my baby is growing fine. Getting bigger and stronger every day.

Oh how I dread to think what Mother is going to say when she learns my baby is black."

"Stop right there!" Lucille sharply interrupted.

She began to cough dramatically, and her voice was trembling. "Slow down a minute girl and pour me a glass of that port on the desk. Hurry before I choke to death Isabelle. There's a love."

Isabelle rushed to the desk and poured her grandmother some of the port, and Lucille sipped at it. She had always been a bit of a boozer, and still enjoyed the odd tipple every now and then.

She began to scratch her head. "Pregnant you say! For a black man? Have you gone nuts?" Lucille sternly asked.

"Going out with one, maybe! But to have a brown baby! Are you losing your mind Isabelle?" Lucille looked disappointed, and Isabelle struggled to respond. She found it extremely disheartening that her grandmother had reacted in that way.

"You know this is going to cause a lot of problems with your parents. You having a black man's child!"

"Are you sure you're ready for motherhood? She asked and went deep into her anti-black speech.

"Is this so called bloke of yours forcing you to have his baby, Isabelle?"

"No, Grandmamma, he…"

"How do you know he'll stick by you? Snapped Lucille. "Does he even want this child?"

Lucille had begun to irritate Isabelle, with the things she was saying. It was bad, and Isabelle felt she could no longer listen to her grandmother speak. "Do you hear me girl?" Lucille raised her voice and said.

"You know your mother is going to do her nut. She's always believed those people never amount to much. Niggers! Or is it wogs she calls 'em? Yeah, wogs! That's it!"

Lucille wouldn't stop. She just kept going on and on!

Isabelle hated when her family spoke bad of black people.

"You'll regret it one day!" Her mother Clara used to say. "Putting those darkies above your own!"

But Isabelle was defiant. A humanitarian by nature, she loved all people, but was extremely partial to blacks. She use to wish she was black herself, although that was more during her youth, than now. Back then, Isabelle saw herself as white on the outside only, but beneath her exterior she was one hundred percent black.

Unfortunately, the rest of her family did not share her enthusiasm. They were quite the opposite, and being bigoted, they deeply objected to the mixing of races. Isabelle's mother was a racist, but not has racist as her father. For William Mason was a man who deeply despised black folk. He had been beaten badly by a black boy on his last day of school, and ended up in hospital for three weeks, with a broken nose, a fractured leg, plus some minor cuts and bruises to the rest of his body.

Up until quite recently William had not told a single soul the truth behind those injuries. It was only after his own children had left home that he admitted what really took place that night he got hospitalized.

All those years he had been too embarrassed to confess that he'd instigated the entire thing. William falsely told his parents some ridiculous story about being attacked by a gang of youths, when in actual fact it was just one boy that had beat the crap out of him. A lad William had bullied in school for almost a full year. The boy finally had enough one day and stood up to William. He was a young black boy called Dwayne Howard, and Dwayne had reached boiling point. He refused to be William's victim any longer.

The trouble started on the very first day Dwayne arrived at Leamington High Secondary School. He was placed in class 5B, partway through an English lesson, and from the moment he walked into the classroom and sat down, William or Bill (as he was better known back then), started taunting him.

Break time was the worst. William and his friends would follow Dwayne around the playground and tease him unremittingly.

"Run to Mummy, jungle bunny" William would say, or "Nig nog golliwog!" This was day in day out. Them terrorising the poor lad, and never giving him a moment's peace. It was almost ritual. There were even occasions when they would get physical, and punch Dwayne in the back or in his face. Poor Dwayne. It was his final year and William made that year hell. Right down to the very last week the bullying did not subside, but by then Dwayne had simply had enough.

On their last day of school, Dwayne cornered William. It was a Friday night, and he knew William and his mates would be hanging out drinking. It was common practice for them to congregate on the Leamington Estate, with some of the other kids from the block.

That particular Friday as they made their way home, Dwayne and his mates lay waited William and his gang. Harsh words were exchanged between rivals, before William threw the first punch.

The outcome was shocking. Dwayne beat William to a pulp. He was black and blue by the time Dwayne had finished with him. William could barely stand on his feet in the end. He had to beg Dwayne to stop.

An ambulance was called, which took William to hospital and from that day onwards William never spoke another ill word to Dwayne again.

Isabelle knew her parents would not find it easy embracing their black grandchild. So she had no wish to inform them of her pregnancy for now. Furthermore, her grandmother was doing her head in, with the venom she spewed from her mouth. So silently Isabelle snuck out of the study, and left Lucille yapping away to herself.

CHAPTER SEVEN

"Cheeky cow!" Lucille grumbled, when she realised Isabelle had left the room. Isabelle had gone to look for her mother. Clara Ann Mason. Who was on a stepladder hanging curtains, in the drawing room!

"Morning, Mother!" said Isabelle.

"Hello, Belle!" Answered Clara. "What a wonderful surprise!" She said as she stepped down from the ladder to give her daughter a hug. "Why didn't you tell me you were coming?"

"It wasn't planned, Mum!" Said Isabelle. "I've got a few things to sort out, so I won't even be down for very long."

Clara looked disappointed. But still she smiled and kissed Isabelle on the cheek.

She had no idea anyone was staying at the hut, and Isabelle was not going to make her none the wiser.

The grassland down by the hut was overgrown. No one really went to the east side anymore. It was Lucille who used to keep an occasional eye on the place. But since Lucas died, Lucille had lost total interest, which is the sole reason Isabelle felt the hut would be ideal for Mur to stay in.

Her only worry was Richard Cunningham and possibly Robert Neilson. Richard was a farm hand who worked for the Parkes, and he was also a very good friend of Isabelle's, and Robert was the Parkes loyal family butler.

Richard was the worker who had cleaned the hut for Isabelle. So he definitely knew someone was staying there. Robert on the other hand, was who she wanted to assist her in finding a mattress.

Her plan was to meet with Richard later that day, to pay him for the work he had done at the hut. But not before she spent time with some of the other staff who work at the manor.

Isabelle and Clara sat in the drawing room, sipping tea and nattering away. They hadn't seen one another for a long time. And whilst they were speaking, Isabelle was trying her best to conceal her protruding bump. But like most mothers, Clara Mason wasn't missing a trick.

"Your tummy looks big!" She said. "Are you up the duff Isabelle?"

"Good heavens, no, Mother!" Said Isabelle. She hated lying to her mother, but could not bring herself to reveal the truth right about now.

Upon leaving Clara, Isabelle went down to the basement and headed straight for the kitchen to look for Robert the butler. She needed to ask him to get her a mattress.

Robert had been working at the mansion since she was a toddler. He adored his Belle, and would often say, and would do almost anything Isabelle asked of him, so long as it wasn't to break the law.

There was a spare mattress in the attic. So whilst Isabelle was in the kitchen talking with Cookie Annie and the rest of the kitchen staff, Robert brought it down and tightly secured it to the roof of Isabelle's car.

Cookie Annie was head cook at Middy Manor and a fantastic pie maker who would spoil Isabelle rotten, given the opportunity. Annie was peeling some apples when Isabelle walked into the kitchen. She was making a pie for the family's dessert that evening.

"Isabelle, my lovely!" Annie screamed with her hands in the air, when Isabelle entered the kitchen. Annie's cheeks and apron were covered in flour, but that didn't deter Isabelle from giving her a hug.

There were three other people working in the kitchen with Annie. Miss Ruby and Amy Teller, who Isabelle knew very well, and there was a new employee; Timothy, who Isabelle had not met before.

Everyone looked please to see Isabelle, including the new guy. Isabelle laughed and joked with Annie as they peeled apples together, and like Clara Annie couldn't help noticing that Isabelle looked a bit plumper around the waist. "Are you with child lass? Annie asked. But Isabelle wasn't giving anything away to Annie either. "No!" She replied. "I'm just putting on weight Cookie Annie!"

Whenever she was up at the mansion, Isabelle loved hanging around the kitchen with Annie, even as a child.

Isabelle spent about half an hour with Annie and when she was leaving, Annie made her up a basket full goodies.

*

I was sweeping the front porch, when Isabelle arrived back at the hut, so I stopped and untied the mattress from the roof rack. *Finally, I was going to get a decent night's sleep in this place!*
I took the thin spikey mattress from the bed and leaned it up against the wall, then I put the new one on the bed.

Isabelle had popped back out. She'd gone over to the farm to pay Richard, who was separating the lambs from the ewes, in preparation for tail removal and castration.

Later that evening and when all the workers had left for the day, like she promised, Isabelle and I went for a stroll over at the farm.

We wasn't there for long, before I wanted to leave. The pigs had become terribly and noisy, which worried me. I thought someone might hear them and come to see what was wrong.

Isabelle and I made our way to the cold storage building. Which was jam-packed with carcasses hooked on metal conveyor belts. There were joints of lamb, pork and beef, and in the freezer area we saw drumsticks, ribs, cuts of chops and shanks. I picked up some chicken pieces and Isabelle grabbed a couple of the shanks, then we began making our way back to the hut.

As Isabel prepared the evening meal, we spoke about the length of time we should stay at the hut. Both of us knew it couldn't possibly be for too long. The place wasn't suitable for any long-term stay. We began to brainstorm places where we could go next. I suggested Scotland, but that didn't seem to be an option, as it was still in the UK.

I had also decided that very evening, I was going to tell Isabelle everything I remembered about the incident. I was genuinely worried about Phiucha's wellbeing. If the newspaper was anything to go by, it was a case of touch-and-go with her, and I just couldn't get my head around that.

I was eager to know if her condition had improved at all, and I expressed this to Isabelle.

Seated, I began to explain, that when I returned home early from work and saw Phiucha standing in our garden with the arms of an absolute stranger wrapped around her, I flipped.

"The guy looked young, about the same age as mine and Phiucha's son, who had been adopted, almost twenty years ago. At that very moment all rational left me. I was fuming, so I ran up to the bedroom, and as I looked through the window and see this guy hold onto my wife like she was his property, I lost control."

I knew it couldn't be easy for Isabelle to sit there listening to me express my love for another woman, but she had known from the very beginning I was a married man, and that I had not stopped loving my wife. It was a fact I never hid from her and probably one of the main reasons why she was willing to help me out. I felt, she knew in her heart I would never wilfully, have hurt Phiucha.

I wasn't guiltless. At all. Hence the reason I questioned Phiucha's integrity. It allowed me to justify my own wrong doing. I had convinced myself Phiucha was also deceiving me. When it was I who had done wrong to her. Phiucha had more than enough reason to cheat on me, and that's why I quickly tarnished her with my own filthy brush.

I didn't even think about the consequences. I just picked up two paperweights, put them in a nylon sock, and silently crept up on my unsuspecting victims.

Dressed in white when I arrived at the house, by the time I'd left the scene my clothes were torn and rippled in red streaks.

"I'm your son" the young man yelled, as he pleaded for his life. "Phiucha, is my mother. She wanted to surprise you!" He was crying, and I had just planted the final blow to his head.

His words were chilling, and still haunts me to this day. I froze in my tracks when I heard that, and quickly fled the scene.

I didn't even remember what I'd done, until Marcus called me. And seeing that article in the newspaper yesterday. Had just brought everything back.

I'd only punched Phiucha once. But it was once too many and it was the first time in my entire life I had ever been physically violent towards her.

Water filled Isabelle's eyes as she listened to me pour out my heart. She looked shocked and got up from the bed.

"I'll be back in a tick," she said, as she slipped through the front door. A minute later Isabelle returned with a newspaper clipping, which she immediately handed to me.

"What's this?" I asked. And started reading it.

Silence fell upon the room. I felt physically sick.

"No! This can't be right!" I yelled. My hands were trembling, and I threw the paper to the ground. "Tell me this isn't true, Izzy!" I looked at Isabelle and said. "Please, tell me this just isn't true!"

I was on my knees, and I held her by her waist.

For my greatest fear had come to pass. Phiucha was dead.

She had died within forty eight hours of the attack, and my son was now in a coma, fighting for his life. I felt weak.

I knew I had left the boy in a bad way. But not Phiucha. And I certainly couldn't believe I had caused either of them any life threatening injuries.

How could I live with myself, knowing what I had done? I did have some love for Isabelle, but Phiucha was my wife. My life.

I began to cry.

"Oh God! Look at my sad existence! Pitiful me. The primitive asshole. Who hides to preserve his own life, after taking the life of his wife! My Phiucha is dead. Laying somewhere on a metal slab. Still, cold and stiff, with neither thought nor feeling. Unknowingly awaiting the men in black, who will place her body in the ground and give the earth an early feast. And there, the sun, shall kiss her for the very last…

What in God's name, had I done?

I knew for a fact I would have to leave England now. Probably that said night. Because the hunt was on. It was out. Circulating nationally. I was a wanted man. I needed to be careful. The cabbie Thomas Monahan knew my whereabouts!

I was panicking, thinking, how the hell I could I get out of this mess. Where could I go from here? Frantically I tried to pack my things back into my travel bag, but I had worked myself into such a frenzy, nothing would fit.

Isabelle looked worried. I could see she felt fearful for me. Nonetheless, she remained calm.

"Relax Mur!" She said to me in a soft voice. But it was no use. Talking to me at that moment was like trying to penetrate a brick. I was incoherent and unable to respond.

"Let's stay here for the rest of the week." Isabelle suggested. "While I make arrangements for someone to take us to France, and from there we can travel on to maybe, Senegal or Mali."

"Senegal ar Mali!" I repeated after her. "Weh you mean by Senegal ar Mali? Isn't dat Africa? Mi nah gah Africa! No way!" I said. "Not me. Me nah goh deh! Ah weh me ah gah Africa fah? Mi nuh even like dem!"

"Why do you talk about your own people like that?" Isabelle asked. She was looking at me with disgust.

But I was in my feelings. "Mi nuh like dem. Ah dat mi seh. As a matter of fact, I hate Africans like a dose of

82

poison! Dem too licky licky and feisty, and dem tink dem is better than we Islanders! Yu no seh nuff ah dem lov call we slave. So weh me ah goh mongst dem fah? Nuh even mention dem nuh more!"

*

Backwards and forwards Mur paced and ranted. After a while Isabelle stopped paying him attention. She knew trying to get through to him would be wasted energy. He was basically impenetrable when he was cross. Besides she had other plans and was going to execute them immediately.

Isabelle knew people in high places — she had friends who could assist her, contacts she could rely on.

Later that night, Isabelle waited for Mur to fall asleep, then she snuck out of the hut and made her way up to the Manor for a second time. Her plan was to get Mur over to the Pyrenees at the earliest possible date. So she headed straight for the study and started making calls.

She first called Terry Williams, who was someone she had known for years. Terry, also went by the name of Lucky, and Lucky used to be a small-time petty robber who would steal from the poor to feed the poorer. But now Terry's life had changed for the better. Around five years ago, he did two major heists: a jewellery shop and a bank job, which he was lucky to get away with. Hence where the name "Lucky" came from, and has stayed with him ever since. Lucky made a fortune doing those two jobs. He was able to set himself up for life and now ran his own car dealer business, had a six-bedroom house in the heart of Essex, and was the proud owner of a luxurious yacht.

Lucky offered to take Isabelle to Calais, for two hundred and fifty pounds; which Isabelle felt was too pricey. She tried to get him to reduce his fees but Lucky wouldn't budge, so she didn't bother with him.

Isabelle called one of her other mates, Samuel Storey. Which also turned out to be a waste of time. Samuel didn't answer his phone. She had three more people in mind, but she had no luck with any of them. Unsure who to call next Isabelle got in touch with her mate Ricky Pilcher. To ask for advice.

Fortunately, Ricky offered to do the job himself. Said he could take them to Calais and get someone to drive them to the Pyrenees. Plus he would sort out their accommodation and set them up with passports, all for a total of four hundred pounds. A hundred and fifty more than Lucky had asked for, but the perks were better. So Isabelle gave Ricky the job.

Ricky didn't have a yacht of his own, but his uncle Vernon owned a small luxurious boat, which Ricky had access to.

Vernon Pilcher (Ricky's uncle), was a tycoon in the jewel trade. He had made a fortune selling diamonds, and because he didn't have children of his own, Vernon doted on his brother's son, Ricky. He had given Ricky permission to use his boat any time, so long as Ricky handled the boat respectfully.

Ricky arranged to meet with Isabelle at Mulberry Harbour in forty-eight hours and from there he would take the couple across the Channel, where a friend of his would pick them up, and drive them to the Pyrenees. They would then stay in the Pyrenees until Ricky got their passports delivered to them. Which should take no longer than a month.

CHAPTER EIGHT

I could not believe Isabelle had left out during the night, to make arrangements for us to leave the county in just two days.

"You're lying!" I said to her, when she explained what she had done. I really thought she was pulling a prank.

The boat was scheduled for Calais early Tuesday morning. Which meant we had very little time to get ourselves sorted. There were a number of changes I definitely had to make, and my appearance was one of them.

I wanted a brown, or ginger, or even grey colour hair dye and a shaver. Plus I needed another set of clothes, preferably an outfit unlike anything I'd normally wear.

Isabelle left out early Monday morning. She had gone to the bank to pick up some money. Said she was going to stop by the locksmith' to cut a spare key for the car, and that she wanted to do a bit of shopping as well. She also plan to stop by the farm on her way home, to give Richard Cunningham the new key, with concise instructions where and when he should go in a couple of days to pick the vehicle up.

As soon as Isabelle returned with the shopping, I took the shaver out the bag and shaved my already low cut hair, completely bald, and I dyed my beard and moustache from black to brown.

The two of us then journeyed down to Southend beach front. We were heading to a store called Woolworths, to get our passport-size photographs taken, in one of those instant picture booths.

Monday ended up being a very busy day, but we got everything that needed doing done, and by 3am the early hours of Tuesday morning, Isabelle and I were on our way to Mulberry Harbour.

As we approached the harbour we could see Ricky Pilcher standing outside his car, but he wasn't alone. There were a couple of security officers patrolling the area as well. When Ricky see us he turned his back as a gesture for us to drive pass. He obviously didn't want the officers knowing it was him we had come to.

Isabelle became nervous. She told me to hold my head down so it would appear as if she was travelling alone. This I did willingly, but after a short time my neck felt crick. I began to complain.

"Aren't they gone yet?" I said.

"No not yet!" answered Isabelle. "Just stay down!"

"My neck's going to snap!" I moaned.

"Just a while longer Mur! Anyway, it looks like they're leaving now!" She said.

The officers walked off, and as soon as they were gone, I sat up in the car and Isabelle proceeded to park. The three of us then boarded the boat.

I wasn't too sure about Ricky. Whether I could trust him or not. But I found a quiet corner and huddled into it. I wanted to keep a low profile. I hated travelling on water. It always made me uncomfortable.

Thankfully, getting to France took less than an hour, and before we walked off the boat Isabelle handed Ricky our passport pictures. I could hear Ricky telling her we would get the passports within a month, and that she could now be travelling as Cassandra Meakes and I as Anthony Mellor, if we wanted to. I was well pleased about that, because a lot of family members already knew me as Tony.

Travelling to the Pyrenees was horrendously long. It took well over eleven hours. Ricky had arranged for us to stay in a three-bed residential cottage, overlooking Martel.

When Isabelle opened the cottage door and we walked in. I instantly dropped our bags to the floor and held her close to me. None of us uttered a word. There was no need to say a thing because we both knew, life from that moment onwards would never be the same. We stood there just holding one another tightly for a few minutes, which was the first time since leaving Liverpool I and Isabelle actually got close. As I held her I could feel myself getting aroused. Isabelle always had that effect on me, she was sexy and fun to be with. But I wasn't comfortable. Not right now. I didn't want to feel sexual towards anyone knowing Phiucha had just died. Yet I just couldn't stop myself. "Was I some cold heartless monster I wondered?

I use my foot to slam the door shut.

"Kiss me!" she said softly, and as our lips slowly touched, she gently pushed her tongue inside my mouth.

I took my time and kissed her and worked my way from her lips round to the side of her neck. I then lifted her blouse and searched for her nipples with my lips. I began to lick them and stroke them and suck them.

Isabelle was kissing me on my forehead and my ears, and had begun to rub my chest. I could feel the heat from her breath inside my ear. It was comforting.

I teasingly stroked her nipples and squeezed them until they hardened.

My balls tightened with excitement, and my dick began to throb. Isabelle was driving me crazy, so I lifted her from the floor and placed her on the bed before I stripped her naked.

She looked beautiful lying there with her small bump.

I ripped off my own clothes as she stared up at me. She started to moan and groan, and with her legs apart, placed her hands over her crotch. I looked down at her plump, wet split. It was pouting, and I wanted to penetrate her there and then. I held my dick in my hand and rubbed the tip of her clit with it, until it had almost doubled in size.

I was tingling all over. It felt great and when I could wait no more, I inserted my solid eight inches deep inside her.

"Ooh…" I exhaled. Her moist, heated love tunnel had engulfed my entire maleness from the tip of its head to its base.

For the next couple of hours Isabelle and I made passionate love, and by the end of it we had both worked up huge appetites.

*

The days seem to be dragging in the Pyrenees. The place was cold and lonely. We had a cleaner who would come and tidy the house daily. She would cook for us. But Isabelle and I struggled to settle. We had made friends with a few locals, who lived up in the mountainous area like rebels. Getting up there was no easy trek, so visitation just didn't happening.

We spent the majority of our days doing very little. A few house chores here and there, but that was about it. The weather had put us off. It was so cold most of the time and I was getting random anxiety attacks that were getting out of control. Wherever we went, I would be jumpy and was constantly looking over my shoulder.

There were moments when I sincerely believed I was being watched. It was making me tense and driving Isabelle nuts.

Every day I would think about Phiucha and my son. I wondered if she had been buried yet and prayed that Michael had pulled through. I still couldn't fathom how one blow to the head could have killed my Phiucha.

"Something else must have been wrong with her!" I kept telling myself. My conscience was beating me into the ground, and my heart ached constantly.

Losing Phiucha was making me realise just how much she really did mean to me. Although I had Isabelle around, in many ways my world felt empty. Cold and dead. Isabelle was lovely but she could never take Phiucha's place.

By the end of the third week, a delivery guy arrived at the cottage with a package.

The man didn't hang around; he just handed the package to Isabelle and was off. Isabelle opened the parcel straight away and when she saw it was our passports, she leapt high in the air with joy and showed them to me.

I cheered. For without sounding ungrateful, the Pyrenees wasn't my cup of tea. I couldn't do another week of *Escudella*; a thick soup made from chickpeas, meat, pasta, and vegetables. Or *Cargols a la llauna*; snails cooked in sauce and spices. I was eager to taste some proper home cooking. Jamaican-style rice and peas with peppered steak.

At last we were leaving France. Our next stop was Africa, which I wasn't looking forward to. But at least it would be hot there, I told myself. Since I was a kid, I had never thought much of Africa. Everything I'd heard about the place and the people was derogatory, and to make matters worse, I once almost came to blows with a Nigerian. I was in my teens and can never forget it.

The man had called me and a group of friend's bastards. He was shouting "you are the sons and daughters of slaves!"

My friends and I were taken aback. We wondered of all the names he could have called us, why slaves? Before then none of us had ever been referred to anything like that. It just wasn't the type of name you would get called. Many Caribbean's didn't even know their ancestral background was one of slavery. As a matter of fact most of us knew nothing about our history. I personally wasn't taught black history in school. I remember learning about the Tudors, William the Conqueror, Napoleon Bonaparte, Genghis Khan, Ghandi. Loads of great men recorded in history, but not a single one of those great men were black. I learnt nothing of the transatlantic slave trade from any educational establishment. I didn't even know such a trade existed until I watched a TV series called *Roots*. It was a real eye opener and made me realise the importance of knowing one's ancestral background. I still wasn't knowledgeable about my history. But one thing I felt sure of, was I really was not looking forward to going Africa. However, I had no choice.

There was no way I could return to England. Not with the British police on my case. They would find me sooner or later. I had to accept that. Whereas in Africa, with its vast land and fifty-four countries, looking for a black man would be like searching for a needle in a haystack.

Isabelle and I packed our things that very day, and the following morning we left the Pyrenees and went straight to Paris. For two nights we stayed at the Land de Bere Hotel, which gave Isabelle the opportunity to do a little more shopping.

Our time in Paris seemed to fly by, and when we arrived at Charles de Gaulle Airport, I felt somewhat relieved, even though I was still fearful of being recognised.

I needn't have worried. Checking in ran rather smoothly. There was just one small issue with a desk steward, who threw our tickets down on the counter, rather than handing them to us civilly. Her attitude stunk but it was nothing Isabelle couldn't manage. She rightfully put the steward in her place.

We walked pass a store and I caught glimpse of my reflection in the window. I was practically unrecognisable, with this new beard I was sporting and my bald head. I had thinned down my moustache too.

The flight from Paris to Saint Louis was pleasant, and when we exited the plane, the sudden heat almost took my breath away. Saint Louis was hot and the airport staff were far more polite, than the ones who dealt with us at Charles de Gaulle.

Situated on a narrow strip of land off the west coast of Senegal, Saint Louis is an island that sits between the Atlantic Ocean and the Senegal River. It is also an ocean port of West Africa.

Isabelle and I had booked into the Dermot, which was a three-star hotel that overlooked the Atlantic Ocean, from the sandy resort of the Langue de Barbarie.

The hotel had a long terrace, and each of the rooms were beautifully furnished with bamboo and brightly coloured African textiles. There was a small cooler in the room; filled with both alcoholic and non-alcoholic beverages.

We showered together then took a nap before descending to the dining area. A number of people were already eating when we walked into the huge hotel restaurant, so we strolled over to the wine bar and ordered a couple of drinks. I had a whiskey on the rocks and Isabelle, a tomato juice with ice.

The restaurant was a large u-shaped room, with peach-painted walls, and ebony furniture. The chairs had yellow cushioned seats and the tables were dressed in white linen with stainless steel cutlery. In the centre of the room stood a buffet bar and upon it was a variety of exotic fruit, as well as a mixture of cultural finger foods.

We took our time and sipped our drinks as we observed our environment. Then we made our way over to the dining area, and sat at a table for two before ordering our evening meal. Isabelle went for an authentic Senegalese dish called *Poulet Yassa*; barbequed chicken, slowly cooked in onions, lemon juice and peppers. This was served with boiled rice and a mixed salad. I however, ordered a large steak and chips. Safe food.

I also ordered a bottle of red wine with my meal, which I alone drank, whilst Isabelle had a glass of freshly made lemonade.

After we ate I bought more drinks from the bar then we went out by the poolside. Deck chairs lined the circumference of the pool, so we found a nice shaded spot and laid back.

I was drinking a fair bit and within a couple of hours had begun to feel a little intoxicated.

I could just about carry our drinks from the bar to our deck chairs. The evening was warm, and some of the guests were jumping in and out of the pool, splashing those of us that were seated around the poolside. It looked fun and was the first time in weeks Isabelle and I could actually relax.

We lay back in our chairs and watched the sun go down. However, my mind could not help but wander onto Phiucha. Thoughts were popping up in my head, which troubled me. Knowing I was here in the African heat, enjoying myself, whilst Phiucha was laying in either a morgue or some fresh grave, tore at my soul.

It was as if I was on the verge of a mental break down I had to repeatedly tell myself to *keep it together*.

If not for me, then for the sake of Isabelle. *Phuicha was gone now,* and *no matter what I did she was never coming back*.

"Let's top up our drinks and have an early night," I suggested.

Isabelle smiled. She knew what that meant. Early nights for us often meant a night of passion. Pure unadulterated sex. I bought us another round of drinks and we began making our way to our room, which was on the first floor.

I'd barely got my foot through the door before Isabelle started pulling at my clothes.

She dragged me towards her and began kissing me, real hard. But I didn't want to be rushed. I wanted to take my time, and slowly strip her naked. I was obsessed with Isabelle's body and in total awe when looking upon her. She wore her pregnancy well, her swollen bump suited her, and I knew those sexy curves she owned would quickly stiffen my already throbbing bad boy.

I gently started to take Isabelle's clothes off and within minutes my boy was as hard has a rock. I could hardly contain myself. I began to kiss her neck then make my way farther and farther down, and as I engulfed her peach between my lips and nibbled at her fruit, she squirmed with pleasure.

I then lifted her from the floor and walked her over to the bed, and laid her upon it. She parted her legs invitingly, longingly. Demanding my touch. So I put my head down. Her eyes pleaded with me to lick and eat more. Upwards she thrusted her hips, and I could feel her almost wanting to climax. But I didn't want her to come just yet, so I paused and started to kiss her passionately.

Isabelle could taste herself on my lips and feel the hardness of my tool, digging and poking her between her thighs. With bended knees, she lifted her long legs over my shoulders and wrapped them around my neck, temporarily locking me in place. Sweat poured from her face, forcing me to stop for a hot minute.

Up from the bed I got and walked over to the fridge, where I topped up our drinks. I poured myself a vodka on the rocks and her a Pepsi with ice, then I returned to the bed.

She was soaked in sweat and her body shimmered in the dark from her water-drenched skin.

I sipped some of my drink, and using a piece of the ice, to gently rub her from the neck down to her breast. I was stimulating her nipples. Then we both started rubbing the ice on our necks and foreheads to cool ourselves down. Stooped by the bedside I placed my arms around her waist and again started to kiss her all over. Then I climbed on the bed and lay beside her, poking and tickling her body with my dick. She wiggled at every touch.

With my soppy wet tongue, I again probed her moist and swollen split, teasingly. "Ah, baby!" She whispered in my ear. "That's nice!"

Isabelle was in ecstasy, close to exploding. Her plumped-up fruit had driven me to the point of no return. I needed to eat from it again and as I nibbled away she covered her mouth with her hand to stop herself from screaming out. Juices dribbled down the sides of my mouth.

"Not yet!" I whispered, and tried to pull back. But Isabelle could hold out no longer. She refused to let me go and held my head tightly as she rubbed her glistening clit all over my face until she climaxed.

I waited for a while then gently placed my dick on her lips. I began to push, back and forth until I pushed its tip into her mouth. "Spit on it!" I said. "And suck it hard!"

I was moaning as I watched her expertly slide her tongue over my helmet. On my back I lay, groaning with delight. She was in control. I had given her full charge of my very being.

Before long, Isabelle had climbed on top of me and was pushing her fat open slit down on my fully extended bad boy until my entire muscle was deep inside her. Then she began to ride me, like a stallion; back and forth she rubbed, up and down she bounced. My hands were gripping her waist, and my eyes were tightly closed. I was reaching that moment of explosion. "Isabelle!" I groaned. *Ah...*

And as all my strength left my body and gushed into hers. I opened my eyes to look upon my woman, when:

"What the fu...! Jesus!" I had to double-blink. I jumped up, and knocked Isabelle off the bed and onto the varnished floor.

I was terrified and quickly switched on the bedside table lamp. It was horrible. I'd just seen Phiucha's face on Isabelle, looking down at me. Phiucha had superimposed Isabelle.

Confused and shaken by my outburst, Isabelle remained still on the floor. She looked numb and unable to move. I could see I had frightened her terribly, and for a second I got the feeling that she thought I might someday harm her, as I had done to Phiucha.

"What's wrong with you?" She asked me nervously.

I was sitting up in the bed by this time, but I was covering my face with my hands.

"If I told you, you wouldn't believe me!" I sighed. "She looked ever so sad!" I said.

Real sad. Like she'd been crying!"

"Who looked sad? What are you talking about, Mur?" Isabelle asked.

I began to stare at Isabelle to see if the same thing would happen again. I was cringing.

"I saw her!" I said.

"Who?" Asked Isabelle. "What did you see, Mur?

Isabelle was beginning to sound frustrated.

"I'm confused!" I said.

"And I know I must sound crazy Izzy, but I saw Phiucha! Clear and bright!"

It was the second time since leaving Liverpool, Isabelle had seen me in that type of state; anxious.

She hesitantly got up from the floor and climbed onto the bed, but did so with much caution, and although she snuggled back beside me, I could sense her fear and nervousness.

CHAPTER NINE

Isabelle was terrified. She believed if Mur had dropped her a tad harder, she undoubtedly could have lost her child.

Just the expression on his face alone, when she fell to the floor, had put the fear of God in her. Accidental or not, to her Mur looked evil.

The couple originally planned to stay at the Dermot for a minimum of four weeks, but their stay was cut short, which disappointed Isabelle hugely. She really liked the Dermot, and so did Mur. But on their second night, a group of physicians had arrived up from England, ruining everything for them.

Mur swore someone from the group had recognised him, and this made it virtually impossible for him to relax at the hotel any longer.

He refused to leave their room, which was the key reason Isabelle wanted to find accommodation elsewhere, as soon as possible.

The couple agreed they would not be staying at any more hotels. The Dermot would be their last. Mur just couldn't face being around people right now. Besides, he wanted to experience life among the natives. Said he was so chuffed by the treatment he had received from the African people since arriving on the continent. It was changing his entire perception of them.

One of the receptionist at the hotel had offered her assistance. She knew a guy who sojourned amongst the different West African tribes, and he owned a Land Rover. The guy said he would happily take the couple wherever they wanted to go. They could hire him for a week. Which was good for Mur, as he wanted to get as far away from Saint Louis as possible.

Neither he nor Isabelle knew where they were going, but Mali was somewhere high on their agenda. Isabelle had heard of the Dogon people and their advancement in astronomy, so she wanted to meet them.

The driver was a Senegalese man named Ralf, who was tall and slender and looked in his mid-forties. Ralf could easily have been mistaken for Sudanese, because of his features. He looked like them, with his long straight face, dark skin, and jet-black curly hair. Ralf spoke French, but could understand English fairly well (although he didn't speak the language).

Ralf was a wise man with an excellent knowledge of West Africa. Namely Senegal. He understood the cultural differences between many of the countries across the Western coast, and was very respectful of each and every one of them.

There seemed to a sense of innocence to Ralf. He was always smiling, which Mur found annoying. "Big man, ah grin like Cheshire cat!" Mur would grumble to himself.

Ralf had brought an advocate along for moral support. His mate Larry. Who spoke several languages: English, French, Yoruba, and Bamanankan (a dialect spoken by eighty percent of the Mali population)... Larry was also Senegalese, but unlike Ralf, he looked it, and although both men were of similar stature, Larry was a lot thicker around the midriff.

Not a very talkative individual, but Larry was a true environmentalist. He loved nature and all things natural. He could name most of the animals and creatures that inhabited the western countries of Africa, and knew most of the plants and the trees that grew there, plus their health benefits.

He was an excellent driver and navigator. Hence why Ralf had chosen him for company. Larry knew West Africa like the back of his hand and could therefore give Ralf precise directions.

Isabelle and I decided we would go to Mali in the end. A two-day journey from Senegal. The distance between the countries was around eight hundred and forty miles, so we did five hundred the first day, and the rest the day after. We could have reached our destination in thirteen hours tops, but Isabelle was struggling. She had been getting stomach cramps. That was unsettling for both of us. Personally, I worried that the pains were induced because I'd pushed her off the bed the other day.

We stopped and booked ourselves and the drivers in a guesthouse. Where everyone got a hot meal and some much-needed rest. Then at the crack of dawn we continued journeying again.

It was late afternoon when we arrived at the remote village of Bandagara. Dogon country. Myself and Isabelle were absolutely bewildered, for we had never seen people living that way before and weren't sure how (if we stayed with them) we could possibly cope living in such primitive conditions.

Mali is northwest of West Africa, and is an old country renowned for its ancient rock paintings. The first ever known empire in Mali was the Ghanaian Empire, which had thrived from the eight century right through to the eleventh century - due to its control of the Trans Saharan trade routes for salt, gold, copper, and ivory. The empire strived until Muslim Berbers converted the Ghanaians to Islam. Prior to that although the presence of Islam in West Africa can be dated way back to the eight century, it wasn't until the thirteenth century that the entire Ghanaian Empire was finally converted.

Mali was also the first country in the world to open a university, the University of Timbuktu. People from across the continent and the world would attend the university to study trade. This included great leaders like Mansa Musa II, *a fourteenth century Ghanaian king and officially one of the richest men who ever lived.* Mansa Musa would often seek advice from the scholars of Timbuktu, to find solutions for any of his problems.

The capital of Mali is Bamako, and Bandagara (where we were), is east of Bamako.

Larry had a few friends living in Bandagara. They were Dogon. And they lived in ancient rocks at the foot of the hills. Dogon's are a special people. Believed to be of Ancient Egyptian and sub-Saharan descent. They are dark-skin and are known to have possessed astronomical knowledge long before modern scientists. The Dogon had correctly place the Earth in our solar system within the Milky Way, before the introduction of the great telescopes. It is well documented. They also knew that the stars are more distant from the earth than the planets, and had knowledge of how blood circulates in the body long before it was discovered by William Harvey in the seventeenth century. And they claim all the gods descend from one particular star, which they could identify and describe in detail. The Dogon believed the universe was born from an explosion that gave birth to the star we know today as Sirius B. They say Sirius B rotates around 'Sirius A' every sixty years, so traditionally the Dogon celebrate this with a festival. Which happens once every sixty years (but only when the star lines up with the Sun). It took scientists elsewhere in the world at least two decades to confirm these claims. And this was after thorough investigation. To date the Dogon knowledge has been proved to be accurate and far more advanced, scientifically as well as archeologically, than that of modern-day scientists, yet to date the Dogon have never had access to, or the use of any technological equipment to assist with any of their findings.

When Isabelle and I arrived at the Dogon village, the people weren't too welcoming. Larry had introduced us to his friend, and the friend introduced us to a tribal elder. We only spent a short time there on the first visit, then we booked ourselves into a guesthouse, some thirty or so miles away.

From then onwards Isabelle and I would visit the Dogon village almost every day. After a few weeks we had rented a house and we had purchased a cheap banger (old car)), so we were able to travel freely. Some days we would go to the village from early in the morning and return to our rented place by evening. Isabelle spent most days amongst the tribal women. They would wash clothes and prepare meals, whilst we, the men, went out hunting.

I loved hunting, and enjoyed gathering honey. I would stand near the foot of the tree and kill myself with laughter, when one of the men got stung from a bee.

Initially, Dogon life was pretty difficult adjusting to. We missed so many of our basic home comforts. But as time passed, material things became insignificant. They no longer mattered.

We began to fall in love with the country and the people. Their humble way of life really appealed to us. They were poor when it came to material possessions, but rich in every other way, because they lived free and natural.

The Dogon had put on a feast for me and Isabelle after a couple of months. A feast that was like nothing we were used to. Dogon's weren't great meat eaters like the English. Their main staple was millet, a grain pounded into flour, which the women would make a thick paste from, similar in appearance to mashed potato, but possessing the consistency of ground rice. Some ate millet for breakfast, dinner, and lunch, but they tended to be the poorer members of the tribe.

On the day of the feast, the Dogon had killed some chickens, which was a rarity but in every way enjoyable. There was body-painting, singing, dancing, drinking, and eating, and everyone seemed to enjoy it.

Strangely, although I hadn't been in Africa for very long, I was already questioning my opinion of African people. A people who had received me well and welcomed me in a way I had not thought imaginable, and that was literally from the moment I stepped off the plane. I wanted to learn more about this indigenous tribe, so Isabelle and I decided we were going to spend most of our time amongst these people, until it was safe for us to return home to England.

CHAPTER TEN

Meanwhile, back in the UK, Detective Superintendent Phillip Jones from the Teesside Murder Squad was leading the investigation of the murder of Phiucha Dera.

Jones had put out an appeal for anyone with information that could lead to the possible arrest of Mur Simon Dera, then they should come forward.

DSI Jones made an announcement on the radio station and on television, making it clear that if people were found to be withholding information, no matter how small, they would be held accountable and charged with aiding and abetting.

Jones wanted to know what had taken place on the day Phiucha was viciously attacked. There were several officers working on the case, and he had sent two of them to speak with both family and friends of the Dera's, to determine who the main people were in the couple's life, plus find out who had seen them last?

Officer Peter Sloane, a short stocky fellow with curly brown hair, and Officer Stephen Cunningham, a slightly taller blond headed man of thin stature, were given instructions to attend Granby Street. A notorious area in Toxteth south of Liverpool's city centre. It was a culturally mixed area and home to a large Caribbean community.

Toxteth was also Liverpool's drug city and the officers were hoping to convince someone awaiting sentencing to become an informer for them, in exchange for reduce jail time. However, in Mur's case, nothing was happening. Weeks had passed since the start of the investigation, and still the police had no further leads. They were getting absolutely nowhere with their inquiries.

Officers Sloan and Cunningham knocked door after door, week in week out, but as soon as Mur's name was mentioned, people would clam up.

The constables had even visited Marcus Cummings, Mur's good friend, and questioned Marcus on when he had last spoken to Mur. But Marcus played the fool. Acted like he and Mur hadn't talked in ages.

"I'm not the man's keeper!" He said to Officer Cunningham. "I don't know where the guy is!"

The investigation was proving to be a dead-ender. Every bit of information the officers tried to achieve fell through, and time was rapidly running out. The longer the case took, the less likely they were going to be able to solve it. Evidence was probably slipping from witnesses' minds, which inevitably could leave the case cold. No one was saying anything viable, and nobody knew of any woman Mur was supposed to be dating. Besides his wife.

During the enquiry somebody had told officers Sloan and Cunningham, that on more than one occasion they'd seen Mur talking to some Caucasian woman, and they believed the woman went by the name of Izzy, but that was about it.

DSI Jones had broadcast this in his TV appeal, soon after Phiucha's death. But the inspector had no surname to go by and he wasn't even sure if Izzy was the woman's proper name. No one from Granby Street had even heard of or seen this Izzy person.

The entire city seemed to be suffering from brain fog, and Jones wanted to know why.

The Detective Superintendent was a quiet man, but not one to underestimate. He was around 5ft 9 and quite stocky built. He kept his greying hair short and wore his moustache thick.

Who is this Mur person? And what control does he have over our city? The superintendent said to his colleagues during an update. These were questions DSI Jones was intent on getting answers to. He knew he wasn't dealing with a common criminal. And for some reason he was getting the impression that the people from Granby Street feared this Mur character.

It wasn't the first murder case Jones had dealt with, but it was the first one that had him totally bewildered. He'd searched Mur's home and place of business, to seek evidence, yet everything about the suspect seemed to be above board.

Jones had found nothing to incriminate Mur. Not even a letter nor a snapshot.

All his tracks had been well covered. Guilty or not. Everything pointed to an upright, hard-working citizen.

Jones concluded, if Mur was doing anything dodgy or he was involved in some bad ass crime, he was a very smart criminal indeed.

CHAPTER ELEVEN

It was six thirty in the evening, and Lucille Parkes was just watching the last of the evening news.

Merseyside Police was making their final appeal on TV, for the search of Mur Simon Dera. They wanted any information they could get on him. Lucille listened to the appeal, and at first dismissed it as just another street crime.

"Another sodding murder!" She grumbled under her breath. "What is this damn country coming to?" But when the detective started speaking of a woman who went by the name of Izzy, Lucille questioned the similarities between this woman and her granddaughter, Isabelle.

Isabelle seemed to fit the physical description of this Izzy person to a T, and they both lived in Toxteth. The police wanted the woman to come in for questioning. But no one at the manor had heard from Isabelle for a few months.

After the news was done, Lucille sat up in bed. The possibility of her granddaughter being linked to such a tragic misdemeanour was inconceivable. Surely Isabelle wouldn't get mixed up with people like that. Lucille told herself.

She was feeling so much uncertainty about this case, and Lucille's gut was telling her the person Merseyside police were looking for, was her granddaughter, Isabelle. The suspense was too much. Clara was the last person in the family to speak with Isabelle, and that was over the telephone. Isabelle had called her mother from France to say she was well, and would be in touch soon.

Lucille was becoming restless. She needed to have a word with Clara — immediately. She wasn't going to tell Clara about Isabelle dating a black man. Well not yet, anyway! Nor was she going to mention anything about the pregnancy. Lucille just wanted to know if Clara had heard anything more from Isabelle, since they last spoke on the phone.

A frail Lucille slowly crept out of bed, and walked to the door. "Finny!" She shouted, and held onto the door frame for support. *Finny was Lucille's hand maid, and she had been working with the Parkes, for the best part of twenty years.*

A petite redhead in her mid-forties, Finny had four children of her own, but she was totally committed to her job, and absolutely adored Lucille Parkes.

"Yes, Ms Lucille!" Finny said as she ran towards her mistress. "What can I do for you, ma'am?"

"Go and get Clara!" Ordered Lucille abruptly. "Tell her I need to speak with her now! It's important!"

Finny turned on her heels and ran to get Clara.

Within minutes, an unimpressed Clara was standing at her mother's door.

"Yes, Mother!" Clara said sharply upon entering Lucille's room. "What's wrong now?" She was feeling a bit peeved, believing Lucille had probably called her for some minor matter, like she'd normally do!

112

"Have you heard from Isabelle lately?" Lucille asked.

"No," answered Clara. "Nothing at all? Not since she last called from France. Why mother is something wrong?"

"Did you watch this evening's news?" Asked Lucille.

"No. I didn't, Mum." "Why?" Said Clara.

"Oh, nothing! I just wanted to know if you'd heard from her."

Lucille was tempted to mention the police appeal, but she didn't want to jump the gun, or raise any unnecessary alarm bells.

Not only that. It wouldn't be the first time Isabelle was away from the family for a long period of time, and not got in touch with anyone. Once, Isabelle had not contacted her mother for over a year.

"Mother!" Clara turned to Lucille and said. "What is it, what are you concerned about?"

"Oh, nothing!" Answered Lucille. "That's all!"

Clara exited the room leaving Lucille still totally dissatisfied. So Lucille promised herself if no one heard from Isabelle soon, she would disclose to Clara absolutely everything Isabelle had confided in her.

CHAPTER TWELVE

It was almost four months to the day we had arrived in Africa and Isabelle was now in hospital about to give birth. The baby was three weeks early and Isabelle was in the delivery room tossing and turning on the bed in agony.

"This is hell!" She looked over at me and screamed. I was sitting by her bedside. "I can't take any more!" Isabelle yelled as she panted and pushed and gasped for air. Her labour had exceeded nine hours, and she still hadn't fully dilated. The contractions were coming fast and furious, and Isabelle complained that her lower back felt like it was ripping in two.

"Please!" She begged.

The midwife gave her pain relief, plus gas and air, but nothing seemed to ease her discomfort.

She was slowly approaching her tenth hour when the baby finally decided to exit her womb. And such a beautiful little baby girl she was. With some powerful lungs. Our daughter let out one almighty scream the moment her airways were unblocked. As if to say 'Yes! I'm here now.' I couldn't help but smile at her.

Isabelle and I decided we would call the baby Malia. I felt so proud. My daughter was gorgeous. Scrunched up face an all. She was beautiful in my eyes, just like her mother.

Isabelle didn't say much after she had given birth. She looked a bit dazed to me. The nurse had placed Malia on her mother to suckle, but I noticed that Isabelle was not interacting with the baby at all. She just didn't look right, and for a second appeared to be in a hypnotic state. Suddenly Isabelle's eyes closed, and her arms dropped to her sides, releasing the baby.

"Isabelle!" I called, and grabbed onto Malia. "Are you alright?" But Isabelle wasn't responsive.

Something terrible was wrong. I knew it, I could feel it. "Isabelle!" I called again. "Nurse… Help!"

The nurse came rushing over, and took one look at Isabelle, before pressing the emergency button. She also took Malia from me, and place her in a cot beside her mother. Then the medics came rushing into the room and politely asked me to leave.

The team must have worked on Isabelle for at least half an hour, and during that time, I was panicking. I had even tried to re-enter the room. But one of them shouted "get him out!" Whilst another ushered me to the door.

I was absolutely terrified.

Having already lost Phiucha, I didn't want to lose Isabelle as well.

Isabelle was bleeding heavily. I saw clots of blood on the floor, and the sheets she was laying on were drenched too. It looked real bad. I felt guilty and that I was the cause of it.

Doctors tried their best, but the hospital didn't appear to be fully equipped. Not like hospitals back in England. After they had done what they could for Isabelle, the doctor asked me to accompany him into a side room.

I want to see her first. I said to the doctor. *I want to see Isabelle. Just to reassure her I'm here, by her side.*

"Is she stable Doctor? I then asked.

The doctor opened the side room door and told me to take a seat. "The news wasn't good" he said. Isabelle had lost a hell of a lot of blood, and had haemorrhaged shortly after giving birth.

How I wished she'd listened to me a few months back, when I suggested she should return to England to have the baby. But stubborn Isabelle refused.

The doctors fought furiously to keep her alive, but the Lord had other plans. Isabelle didn't even get to hold Malia again; My Isabelle's eyes had permanently shut. She had died with Malia upon her.

The doctor explained that I had re-entered the ward when they were trying to resuscitate her. For Isabelle's life had already left her body, and that was practically minutes after she had the baby.

The Doctor and I walked back into the room where Isabelle lay down, and as I looked at everyone standing around her bedside, and saw the doctors and nurses almost reduced to tears, it touched me. They'd covered her with a sheet, from the neck down.

"Such a young beautiful young woman!" I could hear someone saying. Another was shaking his head, pitifully.

116

Silent and in shock, my throat tightened like I was going to suffocate. "I can't breathe!" I shouted, and with one hand on my chest and the other on my throat I panicked and quickly left the delivery room. I needed air.

I started to bawl. The corridor was crowded with people, but I didn't care. I could not stop myself. Some looked on sympathetically, others seemed startled. But that didn't bother me. I stood with my back against the wall, and like a child I cried.

"Punishment!" I wept. "Punishment for Phiucha."

A couple of nurses came to my aid, and beckoned me to follow them. But I wasn't interested. I was too distressed and turned and walked away.

I needed to leave the hospital grounds. To get from this place. Two of the most important women in my life had died, within five months of each other. What in heaven's name was happening? What was I going to do? Where would I go now?

I certainly couldn't stay in Africa for much longer! *Not without Izzy!* My head was all over the place.

Money wasn't my problem. Isabelle had ensured we were financially safe, for the next couple of years at least. She had opened up a joint account under our aliases and it still had over twenty thousand pounds in it.

My main worry was my daughter now. Malia! What would I do with her? I certainly couldn't leave her behind. Nor could I send her to Isabelle's family! People would learn of my whereabouts if I did that.

117

"I had to get away! Just disappear from this God forbidden place for a while! To get my thoughts together!"

Dazed, I left the hospital without telling a single soul I was going.

Not even the two friends that had accompanied me, Baba and Abdul. I knew they would probably send a search party out to look for me soon, but I just had to get away and they were nowhere to be seen when I was ready to leave.

I walked the street most of the night, until I fell asleep under a tree. You could tell I had slept rough. My clothes were filthy when I returned to the hospital the following morning. The hospital corridors were again full of people, so I headed straight to a nurse to ask about Malia. The nurse directed me to reception, and the receptionist explained that the child had been placed in a new born unit. I made my way to the unit and spoke to an obstetrician. He wanted to know, besides Isabelle and me, if Malia had any other family members in Mali, and expressed concerns for my mental state. The hospital believed I would struggle to provide adequate care for Malia, due to my present frame of mind.

The hospital also wanted to know what my plans were for Isabelle's body.

It was all too much to take in, but I knew I had to contain myself and cooperate, or risk the possibility of police intervention.

I gave the doctors as much information as I could about Isabelle's background, and explained to them her family lived in England but were people with a race problem.

I told them I felt the family would have no interest in Malia's well-being, because she was of mixed heritage, and I asked the doctor for details on how to get Isabelle's body returned to her family. I wanted this done as soon as possible.

After we spoke, the doctor took me to see the baby, who was being fed by a midwife. I took over and started feeding Malia myself. It was a sensitive moment. And as I fed the baby and she looked up at me I could see she had her mother's eyes. "Daddy's here!" I whispered, before kissing her softly on her cheek. "Mummy's with the angels now, but Daddy's here!" I looked down at my daughter and could not help but shed another tear.

She was so tiny. So sweet. Isabelle would have loved and cherished her. *How sad.* I thought.

I finished feeding Malia then asked a midwife if it was possible to see Isabelle for one last time. I took Malia with me. Isabelle was alone in a room covered in a sheet, but this time the sheet was over her head. The doctor that accompanied me lifted the sheet up to reveal her face.

I gulped upon seeing her. Isabelle looked at peace. Slightly paler than normal and her cheeks looked a little flatter, but she just appeared to be sound asleep.

All the pain that was on her face the previous day had vanished. Disappeared and she looked angelic.

"Sorry, baby!" I whispered. "I'm so sorry!" I said and placed Malia's face next to her mother's. "This is your momma Malia, your momma!" I wept. Then hugged Isabelle, so all three of us were entwined: Mother, father, and baby.

When I finished saying my goodbyes, I kissed Isabelle's forehead, and left the room.

The doctors wanted Malia to remain in hospital for a couple more days. To monitor her progress, and to make sure she was putting on weight.

*

I wasn't going to stay in Africa without Isabelle. I had made up my mind to travel to Jamaica. So I could live amongst family. Amma, the wife of Baba, who didn't live too far from the house me and Isabelle had rented, offered to take care of Malia, once she was discharged from hospital. Amma already had seven children of her own, and was happy to add Malia to her brood until Malia was strong enough to withstand the travel.

My intention was to leave Africa when Malia was three months. So I needed to sort out her birth certificate and passport.

But life doesn't always go according to plan. Sadly my beautiful little Malia took ill at nine weeks. She had contracted a fever which would not go down, and before I could take her to hospital Malia died in my arms. The local doctor said it was Malaria. Another devastating blow to add to my already broken life.

I buried my beautiful princess in Mali. We had a quiet ceremony, with only a few people present.

A month later, I was on a flight to Montego Bay, Jamaica.

My aunt's husband Uncle Eddie, came and picked me up from the airport, and I was sure he could see I wasn't my usual self. Still, he didn't ask any questions.

"Whappen, Tony?" He said. Uncle Eddie always addressed me as Tony. As a matter of fact everyone in Jamaica knew me as Tony.

"Man cool Iyah!" I replied. There was no feeling or emotion in my voice, just a cold blank response.

I had nothing to really say and was tired of telling untruths. I knew anything that came from my mouth would require some sort of twist, because of my circumstances. Besides, there was no way I could possibly let Uncle Eddie know that I was presently a fugitive and wanted for questioning in relation to a murder. Neither could I tell my uncle that I had travelled with false documents, or that my wife and girlfriend were both dead and maybe the son who I had never known could be dead too. And how was I ever going to explain that I recently had a daughter, who I had buried a month before coming to Jamaica?

"What type of news was that to give anyone?

I was sick to the bone of explaining myself to people. Sick of trying to prove my innocence. I wanted no more of it, and refused to pervert my situation any further.

Losing three important people, possibly four, *if Michael had not pulled through*, had removed any smile from my face. There was nothing left in me to give. My whole being was tragically being consumed, and all I had left was grief, anger, tears, and resentment.

Was I being spiritually attacked? Was God punishing me? Maybe he was for my mistreatment of Phiucha! For as far I was concerned, I had done nothing with the intention to harm anyone, that should warrant such a harsh backlash.

Whilst in Jamaica I stayed at my aunt's, although I could have stayed by my parent's place if I wanted too. Family members would visit and try talking me through my troubles, but I continued to spiral downhill, and before long had started drinking heavily.

I would be up at the crack of dawn sipping away, until very late at night. On top of that I wasn't bathing. So for days I would smell like a ram goat.

People across the District would call me Dutty English because I looked a mess and came from England. They would scorn me and run me away upon sight.

Uncle Eddie and Aunt Mavis were also beginning to tire of me. Aunt Mavis warned *if I didn't pull myself together soon, I would have to go to my parents' home, in Knock Patrick, Manchester.*

Loads of my relatives would come and want to see me at my aunt's house, but I had no real interest in seeing anyone. My mind frame was one of solitude and I desperately wanted my old life back. I wanted to see Phiucha and Isabelle again. Even though I knew I was longing for the impossible.

It really hurt to know I hadn't deliberately killed anyone but was now considered a murderer. Phiucha's death was accidental, and I was paying severely for it.

As the weeks passed, I sank deeper and deeper into a depression, until it reached a point where I would no longer leave the yard unless I was buying cigarettes or booze, and this went on for almost eleven months.

CHAPTER THIRTEEN

It was August and I had been in Jamaica for eleven months. I was really fed up of the constant drunkenness. So I rose early one morning and decided to hop on a minivan down to a cousin in Alligator Pond.

I was alone and needed to get some space from my aunt and uncle as well as Knock Patrick.

Alligator Pond was a fishing village with a lovely clear beach, on the southwestern coast of St. Elizabeth. I knew the area well, for I use to visit the place, when I came to Jamaica in my younger years. My cousin lived close by the beach, and I hadn't seen him since I was in my teens.

Carlton Junior, *or CJ as I called him*, was now thirty-six, and when he opened his door to me, it was evident he was delighted.

"Cum een cousin!" He said. "Jah no Iyah, is long time mi nuh see yu!"

We chatted for a good few hours about the days of our youth. I still hadn't told anyone much about Phiucha, other than she had passed away. I still didn't feel there was anyone I could trust enough to tell them my story.

CJ knew I was going through stuff. He mentioned he had heard about me losing my wife from another relative.

Carlton Junior was a God-fearing man who would always try and encourage people to seek the Lord. He spoke to me about the Bible that day. But I was finding it difficult to absorb what he was saying.

"I feel condemned!" I told him, and got the feeling my cousin knew I wanted to talk, although he didn't press the matter.

CJ just played it cool, and before I left St. Elizabeth that day, had made me promise to come and see him at least once a month. I stuck to that and visited him sometimes twice a month, and as time went by, my outlook on life began to change significantly.

My cousin dedicated hours teaching me about the bible and real-life events. Things that had happened to people he knew.

One story stuck in my head in particular. About a family. A mother, father, and their five children. They had gone on a day trip to Hellshire beach. It was hot and sunny and bright. Everyone supposedly had a brilliant time, and the mother said it was the best family trip they ever went to.

But on the way home, there was a collision, between their coach and a lorry. The coach toppled over onto its side and fell down a gully, killing most passengers on it, including her five children and her husband. She was the only remaining survivor out of her family, and that mother was currently a member of the congregation at CJ's church.

Her story touched me. It was awful losing little Malia, but to lose all five of your children was loss on a different level.

CJ said for years the mother had isolated herself, and it took a long time before she would allow anyone in her life again. Not because she couldn't meet anybody, but she feared starting over. Eventually that woman remarried, and ended up having twin boys who both grew to be successful professional individuals.

After CJ told me of this woman's tragedy, I made a conscious decision I was going to pull myself together. I started to attend church regularly on Sundays with my cousin, and sometimes I'd go to prayer meeting in Knock Patrick.

I had gotten closer to God, and truly begun to feel a lot better about myself. Plus I had also made friends with a number of people at church. But as my confidence increased, my attendance decreased, and slowly but surely the dance hall gradually began to pull me towards it.

CHAPTER FOURTEEN

Back in London, DSI Jones was completely baffled by Mur's disappearance. Eighteen months had passed, yet still there were no leads to his possible whereabouts.

Not a single officer had the slightest inkling where he could be, and not one person had seen or heard from him since the death of Phiucha.

Both Mur's parents were in a nursing home. Alma Dera, his mother, had Alzheimer's, which had developed over a ten year period, and her husband Roland had a stroke, four years earlier, which had left him incapacitated. Roland was totally dependent on others and still incapable of speaking.

Since putting his parents in a home, Mur had hardly seen either of them, so when DSI Jones went for to visit, neither Alma nor Roland were able to give an account of their son's whereabouts. So they could not assist with any enquiry.

Poor Alma was completely bemused, lost in her own little world. She sat twiddling her thumbs as DSI Jones questioned her, and would swiftly jump from one topic to another.

And Roland? He could barely string a few words together, let alone a full sentence. By the time Jones finished with Mur's parents, he had left the home no wiser than he was when he'd arrived.

Three weeks after his visit, Jones received a heads-up that Mur could be in Africa. There was a possible sighting of him. But that was well over a year now, and no one was absolutely certain that the person seen was Mur.

Being a vast continent, Jones was not prepared to send any officer over to Africa unless he was absolutely certain that the person sighted was definitely Mur.

The case had become stagnant. However Jones wasn't letting up. He later learnt that the delay in him receiving information about the sighting, was down to an error that had occurred some twelve months before.

The error was the fault of Essex police, who failed to notify Merseyside Constabulary of a report they'd received regarding a family's concerns for the welfare of their grandchild.

Their grandchild was a girl born in Mali, West Africa, to their daughter Isabelle Mason, a young English woman.

Essex police had accidently sent the report to London, instead of Liverpool, and London police ended up filing the report instead of forwarding it. Only when a new sergeant had joined the London team and was going through some archives, he noticed that the matter hadn't been investigated properly. So he forwarded the report to Merseyside.

The report stated Essex police had received a call from a woman called Clara Mason, informing them of her daughter Isabelle Mason's sudden death through childbirth, in Mali. Clara had spoken to the hospital where Isabelle had given birth, and was told by them that her daughter died shortly after having the baby. But the child had survived, and the hospital sent the child home with its father.

Jones asked who the father was, and Clara told him the hospital named the father as Anthony Mellor.

The sergeant linked these details to Mur's case, because the woman Isabelle fit the description of the unknown person named Izzy, whom the police had been looking for, from the very beginning of their investigation.

The sergeant had got in touch with Air France, and they confirmed an Anthony Mellor did travel from Paris to Senegal shortly after the death of Phiucha Dera, which coincided with what Clara Mason had told the police about receiving a telephone call from their daughter, who was in Paris around those same dates.

The Home Office too seemed to be under the impression that this Anthony Mellor had not existed prior to him travelling to Senegal from Paris. Also, there was no record of him or of anyone name Isabelle Mason travelling to Senegal from the UK or travelling from France to Senegal during that time.

DSI Jones and Officer Sloan made their way to Essex to speak with Clara, and when the officers arrived at the manor and rang the doorbell, Robert the butler opened up and left them in the lobby whilst he informed Clara of their arrival.

Robert then led the men to the study and went to get some refreshments. Clara was seated behind her desk. She looked nervous and tense but got up and greeted the officers then offered them seats. Robert returned a short while afterwards with a tray of tea and biscuits, and as the officers questioned Clara, they had their refreshments. When they finished, Clara led the men to Lucille's room.

Lucille was in her bed. Still looking very frail. She struggled to sit up. So the officers stood at her bedside and patiently took notes. Lucille took her time to speak. She had eventually told Clara about Isabelle dating a black guy who had got her pregnant, and now she was telling the officers all she knew, about the man she believed to be Mur, because she herself wasn't completely sure if that was the name of the person her granddaughter had been dating.

Lucille admitted to paying little attention to the finer details of her granddaughter's relationship and had no idea what this boyfriend of Isabelle's looked like. She told the officers her granddaughter was ecstatic about this guy, and over the moon that she was having his child.

She told the officers she knew of the pregnancy from early on but was warned by Isabelle not to mention anything to Clara, or the family would never see her again.

Clara asked Jones if he *had received any recent information about the child.* Who would be around thirteen months now. But the officers had no information to give her.

They wanted Clara to write down the name of the hospital where the child was born and the date which the baby had been discharged. They asked for the undertaker's details and any documentation that could assist with their enquiry.

Clara willingly gave the police all they requested and expressed that the child was all she had left of her daughter. Black or not, she wanted her grandchild brought back to England. That was Clara's only concern. To have her dead daughter's child with her. The officers left Clara feeling better informed. There was still some uncertainty as to whether this man was Mur, but with the information they had gathered, they now had leads to follow, rather than nothing at all.

DSI Jones next job was to complete a missing person's file for baby Mason. He could scarcely believe his luck. After searching so long for information on Mur. He finally had something to work with, although progress was slow.

In the weeks that followed, DSI Jones contacted Mali police, requesting their assistance in the search of Mur, or possibly Anthony Mellor and his thirteen-month-old daughter.

Jones sent pictures of Mur over to Mali and agreed to travel there once the police had him in custody.

He was going to stop at nothing until he found Mur, he promised himself that. But for now DSI Jones would sit tight and wait until he receives news from the Malian police.

CHAPTER FIFTEEN

Two friends and I were in a pickup truck, and on our way to 'Four Paths' in Clarendon. It was a Friday evening and we were going to a round robin; a weekend tournament, where sounds meet at different venues and take turns to compete against each other, in playing the best and latest music.

That's where I met the lovely Shelly. Shelly Howell was a beautiful woman and although she was a fair bit younger than me, when I first set eyes on her I was hooked. She was so pretty, I just could not stop staring at her.

She reminded me so much of someone I'd had a single encounter with when I was sixteen. Another pretty girl called Patrice, who I met whilst on holiday in Jamaica with my parents. This was approximately two years after Phiucha put our son Michael up for adoption.

Patrice was a pleasant person and fun to be with, but she was not the type I would ever have taken seriously. Although we were both sixteen, I found Patrice very pushy. Way too forward for my liking, and she literally would not let me go until I made love to her the first night we met.

I looked over by the speaker box (where Shelly stood) and waved to her. She smiled and waved back. It was so cute and an obvious heads up to let me know it was safe to approach her.

Slowly, I walked up to Shelly and stretched out my hand "Can I have this dance?" I asked.

She coyly hung her head low and nodded before gently moving close to me. That night the two of us rocked and skanked and bubbled and drank and laughed a lot.

It was nice, and the mood continued right through to daylight.

My heart was pounding when the dance was done. This beautiful young woman I'd just met, had once again put a smile on my face. A smile I thought had been permanently erased.

When everyone began to make their way home, I arranged to meet with Shelly, the following weekend. Told her I would take her to a drive-in movie, up in Mandeville. She lived in Clarendon however, Tollgate. A place I passed through to get home. So I offered her a lift.

We sat arm in arm in the back of the pickup, and spoke of many things. Shelly was the eldest of three siblings. Her mother had her at fifteen, and soon after the youngest child was born, Shelly's father took off and left the family home. Her mother was from Clarendon, but went to live in the States ten years ago. She had taken Shelly's younger brother and sister with her.

Shelly was twenty now, but still lived in her grandparents' house. I dropped her off and went back to my aunt's.

It was proper daylight when I walked into the house, and although I was tired, I took a quick shower before going to bed.

When I woke, it was quite late in the day, so I ate my dinner and went to evening church. I hadn't been to church in a while, and the one I was visiting that day, wasn't one I would normally attend.

Nonetheless I sat in the pew and listened as the congregation sang and clapped their hands. I enjoyed church and joined in with the singing, and whenever someone got in the spirit, I would smile to myself.

Sister Myla, *one of the church brethren*, was so entertaining. I could watch that short thick woman in her turquoise satin dress and large wide-brimmed hat all day. She would be praying quietly one minute, then jumping in the air the next; speaking in tongues. And when the spirit really took charge, the woman would rush down the aisle and knock and bump whosoever was in her path.

The pastor's sermon was about lies and deception, he read from the book of Proverbs Chapter 9 verse 19: *A false witness will not go unpunished.* Pastor said. *And he who breathes out lies will perish.* I sat there listening to him, and soon began to think, could this be a divine message. Before long I was taking the pastors words personally. I thought he was directing the scripture at me. So I got up to leave, in case I said or did something I would later regret. And as I walked out, I mumbled pure profanities beneath my breath.

"Hypocrites," I cussed and exited the church.

My suspicious mind was doing its thing. Every so often I would get these overbearing feelings of guilt, which would eat at my soul. There were times I felt *I can't keep up with this hiding of the truth for much longer*. Because whenever the topic of lies came up, I would automatically assume someone was directing them at me.

I walked back in the direction of my aunt's house, but stopped at some random rum bar for a drink. I began to down spirits, one after the other. Straight white rums. Shot after shot, and the more I drank, the more irate I became.

Before long I was arguing with some punters in the bar. It was pissing the owner off. He was so mad at me, that he threw me out.

"Move yu ass from mi business place, yu ole drunkard!" He yelled as he pushed me through the door.

Unsteady on my feet, I'd toppled to the ground, but jumped up quickly and continued making my way to my aunt's place. My head was spinning like a whirlwind, and I was feeling nauseous. I struggled to focus. Then just as I was about to cross the road, an old powder blue Morris Minor came speeding past. It forced me to jump back and had to swerve to the right, to avoid knocking me over.

"Is dead yu warn dead?" Shouted the driver through his window. He only missed me by a couple of yards.

Aunt Mavis was fuming when I walked through the door. She hated seeing me drunk and began to tell me off. "Ah dis yu leave England fah." She said. "Fe cum ah Jamaica and tun yuself inna pappy show!"

I couldn't listen to her moaning, so I tried to make my way to the bedroom. Nothing looked clear. My vision had gone fuzzy. I tripped over auntie's big rug, which was on the front room floor, and I bumped my leg on the arm of her wooden chair.

Aunt Mavis's voice was echoing in my head. I could hear it loudly whilst I lay on the bed. She wouldn't stop...

"Him was nicer behaved when him was young. Now him tun man, him ah act like one fool!" I heard her say.

I soon fell asleep, and woke with a splitting headache. It was awful. I had a hangover and was feeling dehydrated.

Aunt Mavis gave me some liver salt to see if it would help settle my stomach. But hours later, I was all pained up again and still feeling sickly.

Auntie had to call her doctor friend, to take a look at me. He didn't live too far from the house, and when he came over he diagnosed me with alcohol poisoning. I felt his diagnosis was incorrect though, I believed I had a virus. A bug or something. Because over the next few days I had a high fever and was vomiting. Plus I had diarrhoea, a headache, a chesty cough, and I'd gotten a rash.

No solids would stay down. Aunt Mavis had to boil me vegetable soup, and she made this awful mixture from bitter herbs; cerise and Quassia, which helped settle my stomach. Every day she douse the crown of my head with a bay rum concoction (a mixture of bay rum, medical herbs and spices). And that helped keep my fever down.

It took ten days for the virus to eventually subside, and I had lost quite a bit of weight by then.

As always, when alcohol got the better of me. I vowed never to abuse spirits again.

Being sick for so long meant I had missed my date with Shelly. Plus I had missed a number of other appointments too. Money was getting tight. I needed a job, and I wanted to find one soon. It was almost two years since I'd worked, and I was down to my last one thousand sterling.

I had no plans to return to the UK. I had made up my mind to make Jamaica my home. No one from the UK knew my whereabouts, and I was still living as Anthony Mellor. So I intended to get a job as Anthony Mellor.

*

Over the coming weeks I searched for employment on a daily basis, and every company I applied to, rejected me.

I wanted a job as an electrician, which was my trade. But no one would risk taking on someone without the right credentials. They wanted to see qualifications, visible documents, and certificates. Carpentry was my next best bet, so I enquired about several carpentry positions, but I was still turned down. I went for a shop assistant post and failed at getting that too. I was willing to do anything, even supermarket packing. But all I got was no, no, no!

Aunt Mavis had taken a set on me. She would moan about every little thing. Said I wasn't doing much with my life, even though she could see I was trying. I was really fed up with her and her nagging and promised myself as soon as I got a job, the first thing I would do is leave her home.

My parents' old house needed fixing, so I wanted to concentrate on getting that done.

After approximately ten weeks of searching, I eventually found work. I was going to become a miner for a Canadian aluminium company called CANAC. They were based in Manchester, not too far from my parents' home.

I was a little nervous about the job to begin with, because I had never done any mining work in my life. Plus I was a little rusty, having not worked for a number of years.

Aunt Mavis and Uncle Eddie rejoiced when I told them I had finally been offered a job. But they also warned me thoroughly not to drink whilst holding that position. As the slightest error could cause fatalities

I started work and for the first week was given supervised training, by a much older man name Marshall. He took me under his wing and showed me the ropes. All the tricks of the trade. My wages weren't too great, but I knew the prospect was there to work my way up, and I knew I was going to use the majority of my money to buy materials and fix my parent's home.

Marshall advised, if I truly wanted to climb up the ladder, then I should take my role at CANAC seriously, and not follow some of the other employees.

After that I was good to go. Carrying out my duties like I had been with the company for years. How I managed to adjust to my position so soon, amazed not only me, but my line manager too.

I was staying at my parents' house much of the time. As their place was closer to work than my aunt's, and whenever I got paid. I bought paint, bricks and mortar with my wages. After my shift, I would work on my parent's home until it was time for me to go to bed. That was my regime.

Within a few weeks of starting at CANAC I was able to completely renovate one of the rooms, and by six months I had added another room to the property. I'd impressed my managers at CANAC so much, that they offered me a supervisor's role, with an increased salary, of twenty percent. I saw no friends, nor family. I didn't even see my aunt much anymore.

Uncle Eddie would pop down to check on me occasionally, but that was very rare. The majority of my time, was spent alone. I was totally dedicated to building up my life, and therefore had invested all my time into making my parent's house my new home.

Not even Shelly had seen or heard from me since our first encounter. I didn't want to see her for now, because I was focusing on building up my life. There was no room for distractions, and if Shelly were around, she would definitely have been a distraction.

I had a couple of women I could link from time to time. But they were for personal reasons. To satisfy the flesh. Nothing more.

I made good friends with a guy from work, called Mikey. He was a Rastafarian and he lived in Williamsfield. Mikey was cool and someone who I felt real comfortable being around. I could talk to him about most things, so whenever he passed through, we would sit and reason for hours, and on some weekends we would go fishing early in the mornings, then roast a portion of our catch on the beach later that day.

My parents land was around twelve acres, and when I first started staying there, I got my cousin James (a slim fair skin quiet man) who had been living at the house on and off for years, to plough eleven and a half of those twelve acres, so I could grow my own foods. I had planted an abundance of Irish potatoes, sweet peppers, watermelon, corn and I had put down a variety of fruit trees: such as mangos, star apple and oranges.

There were other trees on the land that bore fruit; such as custard apple, almond, tamarind, avocado and guinep. But they weren't for commercial use, they were for personal consumption as there was only few of them, and they grew nearby the house. Only the trees that I had planted formally were going to be used for mass production.

Although it had taken me a good while to settle into the Jamaican way of life. I worked hard at building myself up, and things were now beginning to feel good.

From start to finish, the house took just over nine months to complete, and aside from the extensions, plumbing and plastering, I practically did everything else myself.

By December 1991, I was ready to move in. But Aunt Mavis advised me to have a house-warming first.

"It's traditional!" she said. "Jamaicans nuh move inna nuh ouse widout bless it first!" My Auntie was fussy, and took it upon herself to start the preparations, for a big house warming.

She was a great cook and made loads of food for the occasion: Fried fish, fried chicken, curried goat, mannish water, fried dumplings, patties, rice and peas, pineapple upside down cake, and some rich, spiced Jamaican fruit rum cake.

Auntie had come down from St. Elizabeth to Manchester, and organised everything. I did assist her a little. With the simple things. I made coleslaw, salad, and a mixture of punches. But Auntie had it covered, and between us we bought loads of drinks.

People arrived from 4pm, and many seemed impressed by how I had fixed up the house. It looked brand new. I had expanded the rooms and added on extra, to convert a two-bedroom purpose built property, into a lush four bedroom house.

I wanted to send for my parents, so they could be here once the house was finished, plus spend their final years in the country of their birth. It was a matter I had discussed with my aunt in-depth, and she agreed to assist me. That was in July. However, when Aunt Mavis contacted the local authorities in Liverpool, she was met with hostility and obstruction. I had asked my aunt not to inform anyone of my whereabouts, nor was she to let the authorities know that she'd seen or heard from me in the last three years.

But the staff at the nursing home were none too please! They wanted more information from Aunt Mavis than she was prepared to give them, and for that reason, they tried to make things difficult for her. They asked for so much personal information; like names of all family members living in her household; how she could support my parents financially; copies of her bank statement, among other things. My aunt felt they were being way too intrusive and the information they were requesting was totally irrelevant. So she stopped communicating with them in the end.

Their antics however, had aroused some suspicion in her towards me. She would often try and quiz me on things such as why I wanted my whereabouts to remain unknown? I would then just make something up, "I can't face talking to anyone back home, for now!" I would tell her. "But I'll get in touch with them, soon."

My house warming was in full swing. Hector B, a local DJ, was playing the music and everyone ate and drank as much as they could. Later that evening, my old raving friends Robbo Glen and Mikey P showed up. They had bought someone with them, but left the person in their pickup. Robbo approached me and asked if I would accompany him to his truck. He said there was someone he wanted to introduce me too. So I made my way to the truck with him and nearly spat my drink from my mouth when I saw his passenger. It was Shelly. She looked a treat.

What a pleasant surprise, I thought. It was totally unexpected.

Shelly said hi and kissed me on the cheek, then I opened the truck door to let her out.

Five foot nine, curvaceous, slim and very pretty. That was Shelly. She was dark skinned, with short black straightened hair styled in a neat bob. Her attire was a white, knee-length chiffon dress that flowed with every move she made and she had on large gold loop earrings, with a matching chain and bracelet. On her feet were white strapped gladiator sandals that gave her an ancient Egyptian look, and she smelt of pure white musk, which was one of my favourite scents.

I couldn't take my eyes off her, and I couldn't help but kiss her cheek again.

Shelly held onto my arm, and slowly we walked over to the crowd. I spent the rest of my evening drinking and dancing with her.

She stayed over that night. But slept in one of the spare rooms. I don't know what it was about her, only that I didn't feel the need to rush things between us. She was my beautiful flower. I liked her a lot. She was someone I believed I could get serious with. I was tired of messing around. It had brought me nothing but misery.

I got up in the morning and made us both a nice big fried breakfast. It was Sunday, and I had to go to Portmore, in St. Catherine, to pick up a barrel of goods from my cousin.

I was driving now. I had bought myself an old vehicle shortly after I started working at CANAC. It was a yellow van. I wasn't sure of its make, because it had a Ford engine, a Mazda body, an Austin this, and a Volkswagen that... But the vehicle could drive, and most importantly, it got me from A to B.

We finished our breakfast and showered. Then we jumped in the van and started our journey to St. Catherine. I wanted to drop Shelly home first, but she asked to come along, and I obliged.

I was picking up some goods I'd ordered from the States. Cousin Nella and I had an arrangement, where all goods from abroad were delivered to her house, and I would collect them from her at a later date.

We reached St. Catherine just before midday, and when we got to Nella's house, her two sons brought my stuff and put them straight in the van. Shelly and I didn't hang about too long, as I wanted to get her home before dark. We sat with Nella on her veranda for about ten minutes and drank cool aid, then started making our way back.

The week ahead was going to be the first week I would be delivering some of my home-grown produce, and I was so looking forward to it.

We got to Clarendon around 3pm, and the sun was still piping hot. Shelly and I decided we'd pop into Milk River spa to cool off before we separated.

The spa was refreshing. We bathed together in one cubicle. But kept our underwear on. An hour later, we were making our way to Shelly's grandparent's home. Which was a three-bedroom house she shared with two lodgers. The property now legally belonged to her mother and her Uncle Terrence.

I walked Shelly to the door, and she invited me in. Both her lodgers, Carrie and Kim were there, so Shelly introduced me to them. I could have stayed a little longer, but I made my visit brief. I needed to get home to prepare myself for an early start the next morning.

As soon as I got to my place, I packed my van with all the produce I was delivering the next day and when I was done, I went straight to my bed.

My alarm went off at 5:00 and I quickly jumped up, showered then headed out. The deliveries went well that day, and for the rest of the week I worked hard at getting my goods to their buyers. Shelly kept popping in and out of my head. I had really enjoyed the time I spent with her and was looking forward to seeing her again.

I thought I would do something really special with her the next time we met up, and now that I was earning a decent wage,

It had to be romantic. But what could that be and where would we go? Dunn's River Fall, I thought. "I'll take her for the weekend to Dunn's River Fall.

The following Saturday, I arrived at Shelly's for 11:00 She had her bags with her, and as I approached the driveway, she hastily rushed towards my van.

She had prepared a lovely lunch for us. Fried sprat, bammi, and avocado, which we ate along the way.

When we arrived at St. Ann's, I parked up my van in one of the parking lots not too far from The Falls. Then we walked arm in arm to The Fall entrance. I paid for us to get in, and for the first couple of hours we relaxed on the beach. Then we took the climb. I got to the top of the fall before Shelly and began to tease her.

"Slow coach!" I called out.

We spent a good time messing about in the sea. Shelly splashed me and swam away, and I swam right after her and when I caught up with her, we would hold each other close, and kiss one another all over the face.

We paddled and petted one another heavily in the water, and we shared ice cream and peppered shrimp, *freshly prepared by one of the seafood vendors,* on the sandy beach.

I had pre-booked us into the Renaissance Hotel for a night. Plus I had reserved us seats at the restaurant for 7pm.

The two of us dined on our seafood platter, and the mood was one of pure romance. We ate until we were full then walked along the coast in search of a nightclub.

Shelly spotted the Jamaco Bana. Where we drank cocktail after cocktail until late into the night and when we returned to our hotel room neither of us rose before ten the following morning.

After our weekend away, Shelly and I did almost everything together, and before long she was spending far more time with me in Manchester, than she was down at her own home in Clarendon.

She was a tidy woman who would cook, wash, iron and keep a very decent home. You could literally eat off our floor. Shelley also did most of the gardening and she dressed well. Tastefully. So several months into our relationship, when I returned from Aunt Mavis and saw her looking dishevelled, I knew something was up.

"Are you all right?" I softly asked.

"Mi nuh sure!" She replied. "I been feeling sick all day long. Mi cyan keep nutn dun!" Shelly sounded nervous.

"Yu don't notice any difference in mi?" She hesitantly asked.

"Not really!" I said. "Your belly looks a little fatter, but..." I knew exactly what she was going to say.

"Shelly!" I said. "Look at me! Look me in the eye! You're pregnant aren't you?" I asked.

Shelly nodded. "Mi nah try fe tap yu, it jus appen!"

"Oh God Shelly hush man!" I shouted. "You're pregnant!"

"Yes, Tony, I am! Tree monts!" She said.

I was so happy.

"I am so happy!" I told her. "You've made me the happiest I've been, since arriving in Jamaica!"

I then lifted her off the ground and swung her around in the air. *Things were truly looking up, and I was feeling on top of the world.*

CHAPTER SIXTEEN

Shelly and I were now living together. She had moved in with me shortly after she became pregnant with our first child.

I had asked her to come and live with me, because I felt she was spending far more time up in Manchester, than she was down at her place in Clarendon. Not only that, it was better for the both of us. It meant she could move another lodger in her grandmother's house, which would give us a little extra income.

We had two children and Shelly was currently seven months pregnant with a third child.

Our eldest was a girl named Antoinette and our second was a boy called Sheldon.

Antoinette was five but very small for her age. She was born premature and when she was around eight months had been diagnosed with cerebral palsy. Antoinette's condition encumbered her physical and mental capabilities. So her eyesight was poor and her hearing weak. She had difficulties swallowing and was fed via a percutaneous endoscopic gastronomy, a feeding device inserted into her stomach via her abdomen.

Antoinette's cognitive skills were virtually non-existent. She hardly moved around and for safety reasons spent most of her day strapped in her chair. She didn't make much sound either, so there were times when I would forget my daughter was even in the house. But despite her disabilities Antoinette was a happy little girl and always smiling.

Sheldon was four. He had delayed speech, but no other major health worries. His language was basic, and he would only use words with two syllables or less, such as yes, no, Mummy, Daddy and so on. Doctors were baffled by Sheldon for a long while, because the boy had no major problems understanding. His hearing was fine, and he didn't have an enlarged tongue, commonly associated with children that are mute.

Not a single otologist could work out the reason why Sheldon's vocabulary wasn't expanding. That was until Dr Robert Mannock started working at Mandeville Private Hospital. He took on Sheldon as one of his patients and after months of thorough investigations and tests it was eventually concluded that Sheldon didn't speak, because Sheldon didn't want to speak.

Although the children had special needs, our children meant everything to us. They were both mine and Shelly's world, and Shelly, *whose mother hadn't seen them yet*, couldn't wait to show them off to her, when she arrives.

Arrangements were already in place for Shelly's mother to come and stay with us. It was going to be the very first time Carlina would be returning to Jamaica, since she left the island all those years ago. Shelly was preparing the guest room for her visit.

Carlina was coming to Jamaica in approximately one month. A visit long overdue, as far as Shelly was concerned. She hadn't seen her mother for almost seventeen years, and she missed her dearly. Whenever anyone mentioned her mother, she would get emotional.

*

Shelly was just ten years old when Carlina left her to go and live in the USA. Carlina had taken the two younger children with her; Cheryl-Lee, who was three at the time, and Baby Nacia, who was twelve months. The family lived in The Bronx, New York, and Shelly had not seen either of her siblings since the day they departed.

Oh, how she hoped at least one of them would be travelling with their mother. But as far as she knew, neither Cheryl nor Nacia were coming.

Cheryl was married now, with a family of her own, and Nacia was at university studying computer science.

Shelly adored her mother, but she questioned Carlina's love for her. From the day her mother moved abroad, Shelly felt the treatment she received from Carlina, wasn't the same treatment her siblings received from their mother.

That day they all left to go America, was the worst day of Shelly's life. The entire family travelled to Sangster Airport to bid Carlina and the children farewell. Shelly, Uncle Terrence, Grandma and Grandpa.

Shelly remembered how rejected she felt when she had to say her goodbyes. It broke her little heart walking back to the car with just her uncle and grandparents. She had begun to bawl loudly and tried to run away from them, but Uncle Terrence was too fast. He caught her by the hem of her dress, just before she got to the barriers, and he held on to her so tightly, she couldn't move.

Her grandmother, although she meant well, tried to throw down some tough love.

"Ah weh wrong wid dis pickney?" Granny yelled. "Shush and tap embarrass yuself!"

Tough love indeed Shelly, remembered thinking. She did not appreciate her granny talking to her that way. She didn't like it one bit.

The journey home from the airport was sombre. Shelly was really upset with her grandmother and her uncle and refused point blank to answer, when either of them tried speaking to her. *How could granny tell me to shush because I want to go with my mother?* She cried.

As for her Uncle Terrence, Shelly promised herself. If he ever grabbed her like that again, for any reason, she was going to sink her teeth into his skin!

Shelly felt no one had spared her a second thought. For no one had consulted her or let her know that her mother was leaving the country to live abroad, until that day. She only learned of her mother's plans, on her way to the airport. Nobody asked her if she would mind having to stay behind. Everyone thought it would be for the best, if Carlina's eldest child remained in Jamaica with her grandparents.

Well, they were wrong. Shelly felt rejected, and the longer her mother stayed away, the more those feelings of rejection manifested. She had never come to terms with being left behind.

To this day, Shelly still couldn't understand why Carlina hadn't taken all of her children with her, to America.

Carlina used to fill Shelly's head with empty promises.

"I'm sending your plane ticket soon?" She would tell Shelly. Over the phone.

But Carlina's soon, could never come.

"It's not fair, Granny!" Shelly would cry. "Not fair!" The child would couch down by her grandmother's leg, with her head rested upon Ms Ettie's knee. "Cheryl and Nacia mean more to Mama than me!" Shelly would sob. "Everyone means more to Mama than me!" She would be crying her heart out.

It wasn't that Shelly didn't care much for her grandparents, and it wasn't that life wasn't nice with them, because they were very good to her. It was just that Shelly did not want to live with grandparents. She wanted to be with her mother and her siblings.

"Who says there is nothing wrong with separating a child from its mother?" Shelly had argued with her grandmother one Sunday evening. She was thirteen. "All this talk that it is okay for a child to live elsewhere, as long as the child is being well looked after, is nonsense! Yu tink it's easy for a kid to adjust, because life says she must? Yu seriously believe it is that simple for children who know their parents to learn to live without their parents? No, Granny, it's not. I love you and Grandpa with all my life, but mi warn me mama! Mi miss har! Mi nah go get used to it. Ever!"

Shelly was shouting and remembers how shocked her grandmother looked, as those words left her mouth. It took Shelly years to accept her mother was never coming back to Jamaica to live again.

Those were some of her darkest moments. Times she wished she could forget. Things had moved on significantly since, and now Shelly had a family of her own and couldn't wait to introduce them to her mother.

Carlina would be staying in the guest room. Which was an en suite at the front of the house. So Shelly was giving the room a thorough spring clean.

*

Time seem to be passing slow as Shelly awaited Carlina's arrival date. There was still one week left and again Shelly was in the guest room giving it a final going over. She had placed some family pictures on the dressing table, with a few toiletries, and two large thick scented candles.

Then she leaned back against the wall to admire her work. The room looked inviting. *I can see Mama right now sitting on the bed edge, chatting away!* She imagined.

The children had gone out with their father that day. He'd taken them up to St Elizabeth to visit Aunt Mavis, and to give Shelly that extra space she needed to finish the room.

It was around 7pm when they returned home, and Shelly was fast asleep. Sheldon wasn't too happy for some reason. He walked in the house crying, and it immediately woke his mother.

Shelly sat up in the bed waiting for Sheldon to run to her. Sheldon always ran into his parent's room when he was upset. He looked miserable, grumpy and being a child of very few words, his mother had to go through her long list of questions, to establish precisely what was wrong with her son.

She soon realised Sheldon was throwing a strop. He was tired. So she bathed him and his sister, then put the children to bed.

Antoinette and Sheldon shared a room, which was larger than the one their parents slept in. It had purple walls, and white skirting, and there was a cot in there - for Antoinette - and a single bed for Sheldon. The room also had a set of wardrobes, two chests of drawers, and a linen basket. Neither of the children had many toys. Just a few dolls, a ball and some coloured metal cars, sent to them from Carlina from the US! But that was about it.

Once the children were settled and asleep, Shelly went back to her bed. She was feeling a bit worn. However, around 11pm she was suddenly woken.

It was Sheldon. She could hear him crying again.

"Tony!" Shelly called. But he didn't stir.

Mur would usually be the one to get up and attend to the children if they woke during the night. Shelly could see he was tired, so she got up to deal with Sheldon herself.

Sheldon was standing between his door and the passage crying and sweating. He looked like he had a bit of a temperature. So Shelly tried to lift him up. But Sheldon was too heavy for her, with the big pregnancy.

"Tony!" Shelly called out again.

*

.

I could hear her well, but I didn't respond straight away. I still felt half asleep.

"Tony!" She kept calling. So I stirred, and crawled out of bed. "Sheldon have fever! She said "Carry him goh put pon di bed?"

Quickly I lifted Sheldon, and walked towards our bedroom. But before I entered the room the child puked all over the passage floor. It went on and on. Like he couldn't stop. I rushed with him in my arms to the bathroom, and held him over the toilet bowl.

Shelly followed swiftly behind, and when I placed Sheldon on the floor, she took over. Poor Shelly, she had to bathe Sheldon again that night, and after she finished, mother and son came strolling into the bedroom.

We placed Sheldon in the centre of our bed, *so we could keep a close eye on him.* Good job we did that because he was sick another two times during the night. Neither his mother nor I got much sleep, so we were knackered in the morning.

Miraculously, besides feeling a little hungry, Sheldon woke up perfectly fine. No one would ever guess how sick he had been through the night. Shelly believed he probably caught a twenty four hour bug. She was so relieved it wasn't anything more sinister.

The week leading up to Carlina's visit went quickly, and on the actual day of her arrival Shelly couldn't keep still. Nerves were taking over.

Uncle Terrence had gone to pick Carlina up from the airport by himself. He thought it would be best that way, as he was doing a job close by, and didn't see the sense in driving down south to get Shelly, then driving back up North to get Carlina, and again having to drive back down South to drop everyone off.

When Terrence's van entered the driveway, Shelly and I was sitting on the veranda sipping iced fruit punch. It was about 5pm and as soon as Uncle Terrence pulled alongside the house, Shelly eagerly rose to her feet.

The sun had already gone down, so it was quite dark. You could just about make out the shape of Carlina's face in the van. Terrence switched off the engine and a beautiful looking woman opened the passenger door, and stepped out.

"Is that my baby?" She said as she looked over at Shelly.

Carlina spoke in a mixed Jamaican-American accent, and without hesitation walked up and embraced her daughter longingly. Shelly looked lost. Like she was being embraced by a stranger.

"Hi, Mama!" She then said reservedly.

Her mother looked almost as young as she did.

"Mi first born!" Carlina said. "Ya mamma has missed you…"

Shelly smiled softly. "I've missed you too mama" she said.

*

Shelly really didn't recognize her mother, who looked surprisingly different to when she had seen her last!

If Uncle Terrence had not bought Carlina to the house, Shelly would have sworn this woman was a stranger.

Carlina looked great. Young and beautiful. A tear fell from her eye as she pushed her hand in Shelly's arm and held onto her elbow.

Carlina was happy to see her daughter, but the realization that she was never going to see her parents again was also terribly overwhelming. She didn't know Jamaica without her parents.

Esther Kelly, Carlina's mother, had passed away suddenly. Almost eight years after Carlina moved to America.

At the time of Esther's death, everyone was stunned. No one believed such a fit woman could die so suddenly. Esther had a fatal heart attack. But worse was yet to come. Soon after her mother died, Carlina's father also passed. William Kelly was heartbroken by the loss of his wife that he completely lost the will to live. Within a year of Esther's death he contracted septicaemia and also passed.

William Kelly had battled with diabetes for more than thirty years, so he knew very well how to keep his sugar levels under control. But he was so devastated that his wife died. When a rusty nail *ran up into his foot one day,* instead of seeking medical attention, William left the wound untreated. It became gangrenous and rapidly spread throughout his entire body.

Carlina was inconsolable, when her dad passed away. She had lost both her parents in a year and was unable to attend either of their funerals, due to a promise she had made her mother.

Back in the seventies and eighties life was real hard for many Jamaicans. An average family could barely make ends meet, and a lot of people were reliant on money sent to them from friends and relatives overseas. The government was systemically flawed. Politicians were corrupt. Party members were endorsing the intimidation of the opposition: threatening non supporters and influencing votes through fear. Innocent people were being killed as Parties battled for leadership.

There weren't many jobs available, and the few developments being carried out, were by noncitizens, or those who had families living and working abroad. It was unfair for the islanders, and this situation contributed to the myth or better still the false belief that black Jamaicans were lazy, incompetent and incapable of development. It's quite the contrary. Jamaicans were and have always been hard working people, that's why after the Second World War, when Germany had bombed England to smithereens the British Government sent for Caribbean workers to come to the UK, to help build Britain up again, because the Brits could not build their country themselves. Many migrants arrived in Britain June 1948, on the HMT Empire Windrush a cruise liner ship.

In August 1962, the Brits gave Jamaica her independence, but the island still relied on foreign capital.

Islanders struggled! The aftermath of slavery was evident. Jamaica had not recovered. There was hardly enough money for people to feed their families, never mind starting up any businesses. So the creation of new jobs was virtually an impossibility.

Poverty had struck Esther and William Kelly real hard. The family could barely keep their head above water. There was no money to live on or to pay for Shelly's school fees.

The only way forward was for Esther and William, to sell three of their eight acres and use that money to send

Carlina and her two youngest children to America, where Carlina could find work and keep the family afloat.

This was why Carlina went to live in America. So she could get a job that would allow her to support the family financially and continue her daughter's education.

Ms Ettie didn't want her children or grandchildren to suffer and struggle the way she had. Therefore she made Carlina promise not to return to the island, with her children, until all of them had received their full American citizenship and a proper college education.

Carlina finally received her citizenship. But that was only two months ago.

*

"Where's this man of yours?" Carlina asked. She was still holding onto Shelly's arm. "Weh ya hiding him?"

"Good evening, mam!" I stood up and said.

Carlina looked me from head to toe.

"Ya look a lot different in person compared to ya picture!" She replied.

I wasn't sure if that was a compliment or a criticism from her to be honest.

Then she said "the man in front of me looks much younger than the person in the pictures!"

I could feel Carlina studying me. Like a text book. It was as if I was being dissected, and examined bit by bit. "You don't look strange" she continued. "I can't help feeling like I've seen you before! Have you ever visited the States? The Bronx?" She asked.

"Me?" I answered. "No! Never!"

Carlina had two large cases with her, so I assisted Terrence in carrying them to the guest room.

Everyone then sat in the lounge.

Loads of reminiscing and drinking went on. The evening was pretty good. We all stayed up till late. Not even Terrence went home. He slept over, and everyone woke to the smell of freshly steamed snapper, okra, carrot, yam, green banana, fried plantain, and creamy avocado, which we downed with a hot cup of cocoa sprinkled with nutmeg. Cooked by my cousin James.

Carlina said she slept surprisingly well for her first night away from home. Claimed she would never usually settle so soon, but had slept as sound as a baby in the guest room.

It was Saturday, so Terrence did not have to rush off to work or anything.

We all sat at the table and ate breakfast. Then Shelly and Carlina washed up. I could see Shelly was enjoying having her mother around. She had said before Carlina arrived that she was going to make the most of the short time they would spend together.

Terrence went home just before noon, and I wanted to go into town. My herd of pigs was expanding, and I was in the process of building a bigger pen. I needed some metal poles and masonry nails to complete the job.

Shelly and her mother wanted to come with me. To do a little shopping. So Shelly called Nicole (our babysitter), who came over and took the children to her house.

Then Shelly, Carlina and I drove to Mandeville, one of the many busy towns on the island, with no rules for motorists (or rules that any motorists complied to). Drivers drove how they pleased. Cars and mini buses were always jam packed and horns were often used in place of indicators. Total and utter chaos and disorder, which obviously seemed to work for the majority. It was amazing, and one of the main reasons I rarely frequented towns in Jamaica.

I dropped the women off at the plaza and drove over to the lumberyard. And when we all met back up Carlina had bought some slippers, rum, and gizzada. She wanted a take away so we went to one of the local restaurants and bought rice and peas and chicken. Carlina also wanted to visit one of her old friends; Angela Fenton. So we stopped by Angela's on the way home.

Angela's husband ran a tiny chicken farm, which you could smell long before you reached anywhere near their gate. It was a rotten pungent stench of dead animal flesh.

"Ow yu manage fe live we dah smell Ms Angie?" Carlina asked.

"Mi nuh even notice it again!" Angela replied.

Carlina took a handkerchief from her bag and held it over her nose. Then she, Shelly and Angela sat on garden chairs sipping homemade ginger beer. I stood about a hundred yards from the women. I was getting better acquainted with Angela's husband, Dennis. We were trying to discuss business.

I was telling Dennis how I used to work for CANAC, but had left them to run my own business: selling food to some of the large hotels along the northern coast. And now that Shelly was on our third child, we were struggling with child care and the running of the business.

I needed manpower. Mainly a driver. And another picker. I was explaining to Dennis I couldn't afford to hire anyone else. I already had one man working with me. My cousin James,

Angela's husband Dennis listened to what I was saying, but gave no sound advice. All he did was repeat everything behind me. I had to wonder if this man was serious, or just plain stupid!

"Yes sah! Yu definite need anudda driver!" Dennis said, just after I had said the same thing to him.

Every so often I could hear the women's voices in the background. Speaking of old times. And I could see that something was troubling Carlina. She looked uncomfortable. I pondered if it was to do what she'd said. About me reminding her of someone. She had mentioned my voice sounded familiar, and how she was sure she had heard it before. The only thing she wasn't familiar with, was my name Anthony Mellor, she said…

163

CHAPTER SEVENTEEN

I dropped Shelly and her mother off at the house, then I picked the children up from Nicole and drop them off too.

Carlina had begun to get on my last nerve on our way home from Angela's. She was watching me like a hawk and it was leaving a bad taste in my mouth.

I could see her looking over at me, every so often. She was behaving like some suspicious old bitch, and oddly, she reminded me of Patrice. The girl I had met in Jamaica, when I was sixteen. The likeness between them was striking.

The following morning I was up and out of the house early. Still agitated by Carlina's conduct the previous day. I tried to keep myself busy working on the pig pen for as long as I could. And when I went back indoors to take a little break, everyone in the house had also got up.

I was feeling pretty moody and kept snapping at Sheldon, over every little thing.

"Weh wrong wid yu, Tony?" Shelly asked me. I had pissed her off, because I slapped Sheldon on the leg for dropping his bowl of porridge on the floor.

"Yu nah gwarn right!" She shouted. "An its di first from mi no yu. Yu ah lick after dem pickney. Nuh badda wid it!"

"Shet yu mout ooman and leave me alone!" I yelled. Then stormed out, and slammed the back door tightly shut behind me.

*

Shelly was angry, but rather than argue with Mur she began straightening up the house. A little time later she was bathing the children and putting them in their Sunday best.

Nicole had come over to collect her money for babysitting, and when she left Shelly and the children took a walk over to the church.

Nicole was a full-time employee of the family. She had been caring for the children since the birth of Antoinette, plus she did house duties; such as polishing, cleaning and ironing. Not only was Nicole on salary, she also worked on demand. If for example the family needed her assistance outside of normal working hours, Nicole was available.

Her day would start from 8:00 and end at 4pm, Monday to Friday. And over the years, as an employee, Nicole had proved herself to be reliable, honest and hardworking, and had become a significant member of Mur and Shelly's family.

Short and chunky in appearance, with a high voice, Nicole was one of the kindest people you could meet. She had a nine-year-old daughter named Candice and both mother and daughter resided at Nicole's parent's house.

But had their own quarters; a self-contained two-bedroom compartment, partitioned off the main house.

The property was within walking distance from Mur and Shelly's place, so Nicole would regularly take the children over there on the days she wasn't working.

Nicole's mother's yard was a child's haven. Mrs Lynette's place was forever full of children that lived in the district. They would come over to play and Mrs Lynette would let them. She loved when her yard was full of people, because she loved to cook. Known for her spontaneous cookouts, Mrs Lynette would feed whosoever wanted to eat. Neighbours brought whatever they could. Anything from meat, fish, rice, you name it, someone would bring it. Free of charge, and when the food was prepared, Mrs Lynnette would allow people to help themselves. Everyone ate. No one was ever turned away. Not a single hungry belly. Mrs Lynette would never deny a soul something to eat. Maybe that's why her cupboards never went empty.

Baking days were a hit. Her cakes and pastries were the finest. Finger-licking. She did get help with them. Some of the women in the district would assist with making doughs, and pastries and cake mixes, and they would bake them in their own ovens, and bring the finished product over to Mrs Lynette's and everyone would get a fair share.

Shelly always said Ms. Ettie had taught her how to bake. But Mrs Lynette helped her become a great baker. Every Saturday, from early afternoon until late evening, people would flock Mrs Lynette's yard and feast on her fare.

The men would bring alcohol and make punch. Then they would set up a domino table and a playing card table, and would use large broken pieces of rock stone and bricks as legs, and they would get a flat wide board and place it on top of the bricks or rocks, and that would become their makeshift table. Music would be playing in the background, and as the winning dominoes came thundering down on the unsteady table the men would be shouting at the top of their voices.

The sound of children's laughter and cries, could be heard metres away, and the smell of food completely stole the air.

A lot of the women present would try to make themselves look busy, whilst secretively keeping a watchful eye on their spouses. It was a grand sight. The elderly, the young, men and women and children pleasantly interacting with one another. Mrs Lynette's home was truly blessed, and she shared those blessings with everyone.

Shelly returned from church and before going home, she again dropped the children over by Nicole's. Nicole had asked for them earlier that morning, and Shelly was more than happy to let them go. It gave her the perfect opportunity to show off her culinary skills and bake something special for her mother.

Shelly wanted to bake a banana cake. Which was her mother's favourite, and some bread rolls.

Carlina was still asleep. Which was idea.

Shelly took off her church clothes and started making the preparations. She used some bananas she had picked fresh from her backyard a few days ago, so they were perfectly ripened.

Cake baking was a rarity with Shelly now days. Nonetheless, she knew her stuff. Learnt how to cook from a young age, with her grandmother.

The house smelt delightful as the flavours escaped the oven. Not surprisingly, Nancy Palmer, Shelly's nosy neighbour, caught a whiff of her baking and decided to pop her inquisitive head in. Nancy always visited when Shelly was baking. She was fast and beggy, beggy. Always in need of something, or always had a story to tell about someone or other.

"Marning Ms Shelly!" Shouted Nancy from outside the gate, with her coarse voice. "Mi can come?"

"Cum nuh, Nancy!" Said Shelly, but kissed her teeth under her breath. *Nancy really got on Shelly's nerves.*

At twenty-seven years of age Nancy Palmer was the district gossip, *although no one dared tell her that to her face*. Whenever Nancy visited, she would always have somebody's business on the tip of her tongue.

"Yu hear bout Jimmy and Rita?" She asked as soon as she sat down.

"Nuh!" Answered Shelly.

"Well, Jimmy beat up Rita last night, sen har garn ah haspital!"

"Ah lie yu ah tell!"

"Nuh!" Said Nancy. "Ah di troot mi ah tark!"

168

"Dem seh im ketch ar wid wan man. Ah bush.

"Deh was kissing. Ah tree time Jimmy clap Rita pon ar foot yu nuh. Wid im big ole cutlass!"

"Ah weh you ah tell me seh?" Shelly replied.

The women sat in the front room talking, until the banana cake was ready to come out of the oven. Then as soon as Shelly placed the cake on a cooling rack the telephone rang.

Shelly took the call and whilst she was in the middle of conversation, Nancy cheekily helped herself to a slice of the cake, which was still hot. And she cut a piece far bigger than Shelly would have offered. Nancy also took one of the bread rolls, which she ate whilst sipping her coffee.

Nancy left soon after she was finished and just as she closed the door behind her, Carlina transpired from the bedroom.

"Who was dat?" Carlina asked.

"Ah mi neighbour, Nancy!" said Shelly.

"You want supm hot fee drink Mama?"

"Coffee please" said Carlina.

Shelly put the kettle on and made a cup of coffee for her mother, and as Carlina drank it, she began to question her daughter about Mur.

"So weh yu did meet this man?"

"Ah wan dance," said Shelly.

"Yu no any of him family?" Asked Carlina.

"Of course Mama!   Im ave one aunt weh live up ah Knock Patrick and a cousin down by Alligator Pond, St. Elizabeth! Dem is good people and dem always come look fe we… And don't forget bout im cousin James, weh stay ere some time!"

"An weh you did know bout im before you move inna im yard?" Continued Carlina.

"Well, nuh much really."

"Tony ah wan funny man. Im private an im nuh like fe tark bout im pass. Seh im ave too much painful memories!"

"What is it, Mama? Wha wrong?"

"Ah nutun!" said Carlina. She had heard all she needed to hear for now. It was obvious her daughter's man was hiding something, and if that was the case, he was going to be a problem. A very big problem indeed.

CHAPTER EIGHTEEN

Carlina was up and dressed, sitting in the front room waiting on Terrence. He was coming to get her and Shelly to take them down to Clarendon. They were going to visit her parent's graves. Which was in a private cemetery, on a small patch of land at the back of the family home.

Carlina also wanted to check on the house to see what repairs needed doing. She planned to give the entire place a full make over, before she returned to the States.

Terrence arrived by 8:00 and they were off.

When they got to Clarendon they walked around the side of the house, which led you straight into the back yard. Immediately Carlina's eyes caught glimpse of her parents' tombstones and she began to cry. Carlina was gutted that she hadn't been able to attend their funerals. It hurt deeply.

She remembered when her mother died, her father basically demanded that she honour Ms Ettie's wish and not return to Jamaica until she received her US citizenship. It was a decision Carlina had found very difficult to make. But she did not what to break the promise she'd made to her mother. Oh she so wished she had ignored her father.

The graves looked clean. Well kept. They were both painted white and lay side by side under her mother's custard apple tree. Ms. Ettie's favourite spot.

Carlina read aloud the engravings:

In loving memory of a beautiful wife. A great mother and a wonderful grandmother. Mrs Esther Juanita Kelly, born May 7th 1923 and died suddenly July 12th 1984.

"Oh, Mamma!" Carlina cried. "I did it! I got my citizenship and my qualification like ya wanted me too!" She then stepped over to her father's stone.

Again she read allowed the engravings. *"William Arnold Kelly. A great husband, father and grandfather. Born 17th March 1920. Died 21rd April 1985. He will be sadly missed.*

Carlina stood between the stones and said a little prayer. She had bought a flask of rum with her, which she opened and poured over each of the graves and lit two incense sticks and placed one each on her mother and her father's stones. Shelly in the meantime had walked over to a flower bed and snipped a few blossoms. Which she laid on top of the graves. Both Shelly and her mother became emotional.

The family then sang 'Amazing Grace' and read a verse from the bible before they made their way to the house.

Terrence could feel the depth his sister's grief. He knew her pain was greater than his own, because he'd already mourn the loss of their parents soon after they passed. Plus, he felt fortunate he was able to spend time with them, during their final days.

When they entered the house Shelly introduced Carlina to the lodgers, and before long Carlina was walking around the property taking notes of all the things that

172

needed doing. There were a few cracks here and there and a little plastering required. The bathroom was in need of a new shower, and the kitchen cupboards needed replacing. But overall there wasn't a great amount of work that needed doing.

Carlina had arranged to meet up with an old neighbour that day, Marcel Brown, who had kept in touch with her since she left the island all those years ago. Marcel would call Carlina regularly and update her on anything that was happening in the district. But this was soon to stop.

Marcel was shipping out. He was immigrating, and very soon. So he was selling some of his land, to make money for his new life, and Carlina was going to be his first official buyer.

Carlina wanted the land as collateral for her children and husband. That wasn't to say she didn't have land of her own. For Ms Ettie and Mas Willy had left their two children five acres and a house between them.

Marcel was immigrating to England in less than a year, and therefore pretty eager to make as much money as he could before going.

He wanted to sell three quarters of his parent's twenty acres. They were elderly now, and not able to maintain the amount of land they owned. He was looking for a quick sale, so Carlina was getting her portion at a discount. Two thirds of the original asking price.

Marcel had been trying to sell the land for quite some time, without success. Consequently when Carlina made him an offer, it was too good to turn down. She wanted four acres at $3,000 US an acre instead of the $4,500 he had originally asked for.

The deal was more or less already closed. Carlina's husband Clemence had completed the sale from America. All Carlina had to do was sign the deed with a witness present and hand over the $12,000 cheque.

The solicitor was meeting them later that afternoon.

*

Carlina and Marcel met with the solicitor as planned, and the paperwork was signed. Everything went accordingly. So by the time they were heading back to Manchester, Carlina and her husband were the legal owners of four acres of unspoilt Clarendon land. Lush and green and ready to cultivate.

She had always been fortunate in life (Carlina). Including with men. She had met a remarkable young man, who married her after only being in America for two years.

Clemence was a barber by trade, and owned a chain of saloons in and around the Bronx area. He had pushed Carlina to purchase Marcel's land, and between them raised $30,000 US to clear the area and put a property upon it. Clemence wanted to build a foundation away from the States. For in his opinion, America wasn't doing right by a number of its black citizens.

The gang scene was rising, and the mistreatment of blacks was getting out of control. Police were brutalizing them. Killing them and getting away with it. The lives of young black men was mostly at risk, and the lives of the poor, and for those who didn't lose their lives, they were unfairly incarcerated. Given long sentences for minor offences, and sometimes for no offence at all. There were many race riots and a lot of businesses in black neighbourhoods were owned by almost every other nation besides blacks. Drugs were being infiltrated on their streets, in their communities, specifically aimed at the needy. Clemence felt as if he was being stifled. He feared the Jim Crow laws were making a rapid comeback. He was born in the US but didn't feel like he belonged in the US. Clemence could not see how he could ever truly own anything on American soil. For successful blacks were rarely permitted to live in peace. He believed racism in the US was still very much alive.

Clemence got four acres of Marcel's land surveyed months before Carlina went to Jamaica. He wanted to build a ten-bedroom guest house on it. Plus grow cashews.

Labour was cheap in Jamaica, and Mr Forester, a local builder, was going to oversee the entire project for the Chandlers. Forester had his team of twenty ready and waiting, and Clemence wanted them to start work as soon as possible.

Carlina would supervise the project and when she returned to the US Clemence would take over. By liaising with Forester on the Phone.

*

Carlina's time on the island was speedily running out. She had visited a few relatives whilst there, but most of her days were spent between Manchester and Clarendon. Back and forth, ensuring the foundation of the guest house was getting done, and the decorating of her parent's place was being completed. The rest of Carlina's time was used up with Shelly and the children, and although she was missing her husband, she was enjoying Jamaica. And she was loving her time with her grandchildren.

Antoinette had stolen her heart, partly because of her disabilities. Carlina felt compassionate towards her. She would remove the child from her wheelchair and allow Antoinette to feel her way around the room. And whenever Carlina went out, as soon as she returned Antoinette would bang her chair with her hands and turn her head in search of her grandmother. Antoinette could always sense her grandmother's presence.

Nonetheless, Carlina had concerns about Antoinette's condition. No one in her family had ever suffered from cerebral palsy before, so how had her granddaughter inherited this illness.

She asked Shelly if she knew whether any of Mur's relatives had that condition, but as far as she knew, none of them did. Hearing this only magnified Carlina's suspicions.

Carlina knew something just wasn't right. It didn't feel right. Were the deeds of her past coming to haunt her? Carlina prayed she was wrong, but for some reason she didn't think she was.

CHAPTER NINETEEN

It was Carlina's last Sunday in Jamaica and her send-off had been organised for later that afternoon. More than fifty guests had been invited and she was really looking forward to it. To tell the truth Carlina's leaving date, couldn't have come quick enough for Mur. He wanted her gone, out of his home, back on a plane heading to New York and out of his life. Having her around hadn't been easy. Her presence put him on edge. Mur was having thoughts that he shouldn't be having and he couldn't help thinking this woman had come to Jamaica to ruin his life. That morning everyone – excluding Mur – was getting ready to go church.

Carlina still hadn't spoken to him about her concerns as yet. She wanted to do it directly, face to face, when they were alone.

Shelly, Carlina and the children made their way to church. The sermon was pleasant and at the end of service Pastor asked if anyone needed prayers they should come forward. Carlina quickly grabbed Antoinette's wheelchair, and pushed it up to the altar. Then she knelt down beside it.

The Pastor put his hand on Antoinette's head and began to pray. He did the same for Carlina and whilst he was praying for her, Carlina said a quiet prayer to herself. She asked God for forgiveness, of any transgression she may have committed in the past.

Why had she listened to Jerry? The father of her children. She should never have agreed with him to keep the truth from everyone! What kind of disgrace was going to befall her? Those were the type of thoughts going through Carlina's head at church that morning.

It would take more than a single prayer from the pastor to clear the mess that is about to erupt. She told herself. Carlina believed only a miracle could suffice.

After church the family said their goodbyes to the congregation, and Shelly invited some of the brethren to celebrate them later up at the house.

Mur was in the back yard when they returned, and he had lit the jerk pan. He'd also made up a wood fire, and upon it was a ginormous pot of mannish water (cow cud soup), simmering away. The women put on their aprons and took over from Mur. There was chicken and fish roasting in the pan. Carlina made curried goat and Shelly done some rice, and the vegetables.

The turnout was good. People from Clarendon, Portmore, Kingston, and St. Elizabeth came. People who Carlina hadn't seen in years tuned up. Shelly had arranged it all behind her mother's back. Some came to give, others came to take. There were a few who would have stripped Carlina of her underwear, had she not put her foot down.

"Nothing more!" Carlina said to an old time school friend before running the woman from her room. Linda Carter was rummaging through Carlina's stuff like the things belonged to her!

Carlina had no choice but to usher Linda out and lock the door.

People ate and drank till their bellies were full, and everyone appeared to be having a good time. A little dancing went on into the night, but by 10pm, the last of the guests were leaving.

Only Nicole, *the children's carer*, stayed behind. She filled her doggy bag and helped to clean up.

By midnight everyone was in their beds.

*

I was the first one to get up the next morning. Carlina's flight was scheduled for the afternoon. So we had a long day ahead. Shelly had asked me to wake her when I got up but when I looked over and saw she *was still asleep,* I just couldn't. Carlina's send-off had knocked the stuffing out of her. Plus with the baby being due in just a couple of weeks, I thought it would be best if Shelly got as much rest as possible.

I tended to the children and made ackee and salt fish with fried dumpling for everyone's breakfast. Then I checked to see if Carlina's luggage was still in the hall. She had packed them from Saturday night, to ensure she didn't leave anything behind.

Her plane was due to leave for 2pm, so I went to wake her at 8:00. "Time to get up!" I tapped her door and said.

"Who is that?" She asked. "Come in!"

Hesitantly, I entered the room and saw her sitting upright in bed.

"Morning, Ms. Carlina!" I stammered. "It's time to get up now!" She made me nervous, and I was sure she knew she was having that effect on me.

"Is anyone besides you up yet?" Carlina asked.

"Just you, me and the children at the moment" I replied. Then I went to leave the room.

"Hold up!" Carlina said. "Close the door for a minute, I need a word."

Obediently I did as requested. But my stomach was in knots. "What the hell did this woman want to talk about now?" I wondered.

Carlina stared at me piercingly as I shut the door and rested my back up against it. She looked a bit nervous too. Unsure of what she was going to say, or how to say it.

"I've been dying for the opportunity to speak with you alone," She started.

"Firstly, I want to know 'do you intend to marry my daughter?"

I was a bit stunned by her question. I hadn't expected her to come out with anything like that.

"Yes! That is my intention" I replied awkwardly. "I was thinking maybe in a year or two."

"That's good," said Carlina, then she began to question me about my family both here and back in England. Carlina spoke softly, which made me think, maybe I was wrong about her. She didn't seem to know or express any interest in anything concerning Phiucha.

I began to feel a little more relaxed. But what a premature judgement I had made. Carlina then threw the hand grenade. "Are you known by any other name?" She asked. That stopped me in my tracks immediately. I tried to but couldn't get a word out.

"No!" I then stammered after a short while.

It seemed like Carlina was trying to pick my mouth. I again wondered if she knew anything about Phiucha. My heart began to race.

"Do you have any relatives —?" But before she could finish there was a loud bang at the door.

"Carlina!" Terrence shouted from outside. "Yu up yet sis?"

Thank goodness! I thought. Saved by the bell. Terrence had come to my rescue just in the nick of time.

"Yeah man, mi up, Terrence!" She shouted back.

It was time for me to leave, *as far as I was concerned*.

I quickly opened the door and bolted. I didn't want to hear another word from that woman, and was now hundred percent sure she knew something about Phiucha.

Terrence wanted Carlina's flight details, I could hear him asking for them, but Carlina wanted Terrence to see if the fried fish, and bami she had put in the fridge before she went to her bed, was still there.

"We got importent tings fe sort out," I heard Terrence say as he made his way to the kitchen "an yu ah ask mi bout bami! Weh yu warn me fe do wid dem?" He shouted.

"Put dem in one scandal and khar dem come!" Carlina yelled back.

Carlina still hadn't finished with me yet. I felt she deliberately sent Terrence into the kitchen, so she could continue with the questions. So I got the children and took them straight over to Nicole's, who was keeping them for the day.

Shelly was tearful on the way to the airport and Carlina seemed to be on edge. She was seated in the back of the van and the look on her face was one of despair. Something seemed to be troubling her. It was obvious, and I was thinking maybe it's because she didn't know enough about the man that was living with her daughter.

Things probably didn't sit right after we spoke this morning. I believed she knew I was hiding something and was determined to find out what it was.

We arrived at the airport for noon, which gave Carlina two hours to book in.

Terrence parked up the van, and Carlina suggested Shelly accompany him to get a trolley for her luggage. She obviously wanted to ask me more questions.

"You know you remind me of someone!" She said. "Do you know anybody by the name of Mur?"

I was dumbstruck.

"Mur!" I repeated. "What kind of name is that? I've never even heard the name Mur before!" I lied.

"Who would name their pickney soh?" I laughed nervously. Trying to sound convincing.

"Well if you're not him, you sure have a doppelgänger out there!" Carlina said.

Thank God! I thought and breathed a sigh of relief. Carlina was finally beginning to believe me, or she was at least pretending she believed.

Intrigued, I wanted to find out what she knew about me, now that I'd made her uncertain as whether I was the man she thought was Mur.

"Carlina!" I shamelessly asked. "What is troubling you?"

"Oh, nothing really." Was her smart response. Carlina wasn't giving anything away.

Shelly and Terrence returned with the trolley, and Terrence packed Carlina's bags onto it.

Then we made our way up to the check-in desk and booked Carlina on her flight. She was one of the first in line and got seen to straight away.

Shelly whispered to me that watching her mother about to leave was bringing back so many memories. She was finding it difficult not to cry. It was reminiscent of her childhood.

"Mama! Yu nuh even gone yet but already me ah miss yu!" Shelly said to Carlina.

We hung around the airport for a little while and when the time had arrived for Carlina to leave, mother and daughter kissed one another then waved each other good bye, until Carlina was completely out of sight.

The journey back home was quiet, and when we got to the district, Shelly had begun to get twinges. Our baby was due in less than a week, so we knew the child could come at any time.

Terrence dropped us home, but didn't hang about. Shelly walked in the house and immediately laid down on the sofa. She was in quite a bit of discomfort but said she didn't feel ready to go hospital yet, just in case it was a false alarm.

CHAPTER TWENTY

A couple of hours had passed since we got back, and Shelly was still asleep on the sofa.

I had spent most of my time in the armchair, keeping a close eye on her. My thoughts kept running on Carlina and the things she had said. It suddenly all began to make sense. *But it wasn't possible!* I told myself.

Finally I had worked out how Carlina knew me. The puzzle was slowly piecing itself together, and it was scary. *What if my conclusions were correct? What would this mean?*

I urgently needed clarity. I had to speak with Carlina again. But I wasn't going to do it from the house. I would call her from elsewhere. There were a few deliveries I had to do up north in a couple of days, so I would call her from there.

That's when I'll do it! I told myself. *I'll call Carlina when I next go up north.*

It was getting late into the night, and Shelly was still sleeping. She looked relaxed, and I could see she was no longer in any pain, so I took a walk over to our local rum bar.

The bar was practically across the road from our house, and when I got there, only a handful of people were about. Which suited me fine. I wasn't feeling very sociable that evening.

"A Pepsi please!" I ordered from the bartender, and sat by the window to drink it alone. I knew most people in there that night, but wasn't saying a word to anyone. I was deep in thought.

Robin, the guy who owned the bar, could see I was aloof, because normally I would be chatting away and boasting about my haves and have-nots.

"What's up man?" He approached me and asked.

Robin and I had become good friends over the last couple of years.

"Mi aright sah!" I snapped. My response was abrupt, unwarranted and I caught myself and quickly apologised. "Look Robin!" I began to explain. "I'm sorry. It's not you, it's me. I got a lot on my mind!"

Robin was cool and told me not to worry, then he left me alone to drink my soda. When I finished I returned to the bar to order another one. But bought a Wray and Nephew instead.

A part of me wished I hadn't worked things out. My findings were going to be destructive. I believed now Carlina and Patrice were the same person, I had come to that conclusion. I was absolutely certain. It was the only explanation for Carlina's bizarre behaviour. Even her voice sounded the same, just a little huskier, which was inevitable with age. She probably wanted to tell Shelly about our single encounter. To spoil things between us! I felt...

Only after I looked into the situation carefully, did it dawn on me that Carlina could possibly be Patrice. Her knowing my name was the giveaway, because aside from

Aunt Mavis, very few people knew me as Mur. I told my aunt some cock and bull story that someone had stolen my documents back in England, and was using my identity to do bad things. I also told her I changed my name by deed poll years ago, because the English police would not stop harassing me because of it.

There was only a handful of people in Jamaica who knew me by Mur. Those were people I had met in my youth, whilst holidaying with my parents. And Patrice happened to be one of them.

Everybody else knew me as either Tony or of late Anthony Mellor.

Carlina had to be Patrice and if that was so, then what was her intention? Did she plan on telling Shelly about our little rendezvous? What would that achieve? It was a one-night stand that happened years ago, for god sake! Why doesn't that woman just let sleeping dogs lie? What is she thinking? If she spills the beans that could break Shelly's heart. I didn't want Shelly knowing anything!"

I began to brainstorm, and was jumping from one scenario to another.

"Oh MY GOD!" I thought aloud, this woman could destroy everything.

Shelly was up and about when I walked in the house. "Tony ah yu dat?" She shouted when I stepped through the front door.

"Yes, babes!" I answered.

She hadn't too long come out of the bath. Said she was still having minor twinges in her back. But the pain had subsided and was far less hurtful now than it had been earlier.

I could smell food so I walked into the kitchen to see what was cooking. It was my favourite. Stewed peas and rice, which is stewed pig's tail, salted beef, kidney beans, and spinners - *small elongated dumplings* – cooked in coconut milk or cream, and sometimes both.

It was a late dinner, but Shelly and I sat on the sofa and ate off serving trays.

I still could not stop thinking about the possible doom and gloom that was yet to come. I looked over at my beautiful woman and wondered whether I was going to lose her soon, due to some careless encounter I had during my youth! I didn't want to lose Shelly. She and the kids had been my world since Phiucha, Isabelle and baby Malia were taken from me. My current family had given me a new lease of life, so much to live for…

I wasn't sure about Michael, whether he died or was still alive. But I often thought of him, and the horrible condition I'd left him in. It made my skin crawl.

Karma was coming? I could feel it. Coming to get me. To break down the life I had worked so hard at rebuilding. I could barely sleep a wink that night, and for the next two nights it was the same. I was up by 5:00 Thursday morning, and it took me less than an hour for me to pack the van. As soon as I was done I headed out and was on my way to the North Coast. Neither Shelly nor the children were awake when I left the house. Thank goodness. I didn't want to face them.

My first delivery was in Falmouth, then I went to St. Anne's. I had several contracts with some of the larger hotels along the northern coast. As my customers demanded good wholesome unblemished foods, and I had earned the reputation of being a reliable business person, and a provider of good quality products.

It would usually take me around two hours and forty minutes to get to the north. But I had done the journey in two hours and fifteen minutes flat that morning. Probably because I was speeding most of the way.

When I hit Ocho I went straight to Perry's Seafood Restaurant, then over to Ital Grill, then Liberty's Diner, and to Destiny's Foods. I delivered to another twelve hotels and guest houses further along the coast, before I made my final stop, at the Maryland.

The Maryland was a posh five-star hotel and restaurant that I always delivered to last. Because it allowed me to spend time with a woman I had recently become closely acquainted to. Her name was Avril Summer and I loved messing about with Avril before I headed back home.

She was a house supervisor at the Maryland, and we had become intimate during the last six months. Women were my weakness. I couldn't keep away from them. I would drop off the hotel's orders, then me and Avril would sneak into one of the vacant hotel rooms for a little rumpy pumpy.

Avril knew all about Shelly, but she didn't care because she was married, to a man named Kenneth.

Kenneth Summer rarely spent time in Jamaica. He lived abroad. In Cardiff, Wales, and although he and Avril loved each other, they had inevitably grown apart. When Kenneth first left Jamaica, he would spend six months in Wales and six months on the island. But as time passed, the months became years, and now Kenneth only visited Jamaica a few weeks every two to three years.

Avril explained to me that she and Kenneth never discussed their situation. They seem to have an understanding between them. An acceptance, that neither wanted complete closure. And although it was obvious they were both seeing other people, none would ever openly disrespect the other. Kenneth had his woman in Wales but he would never travel to Jamaica with her, and Avril would not have any man contacting or visiting her whilst her husband was on the island.

Avril and I entered the hotel room and made love, and before I started my journey home, I stopped by the telephone exchange and made the dreaded call to Carlina.

Carlina's phone rang out the first time. So I rang the number again and she answered the phone.

"Good day, Ms Carlina!" I said. "It's me … Tony!"

"Oh… Hi, Tony, how you doing?" She sounded surprised. "What's up? Has Shelly had the baby yet?" She asked.

190

"No, mam! I called because I was thinking about what you said the day you left. It's been playing on my mind!" I said.

"What is that? Asked Carlina. "I said many things before I left! Remind me please!"

"Do you know someone name Patrice?" I asked.

There was silence for a moment.

"I met a young girl in my youth," I explained, "who introduced herself to me as Patrice. I was visiting Jamaica with my parents, and I had just turned seventeen. Anyway, this girl and I made love the same night and I remember telling her my name was Mur. I had heard sometime later that Patrice wasn't really her name, but an alias she would occasionally use."

There was a noise, like the phone had dropped.

"Carlina!" I called. "Are you still there?"

But there was no answer! No reply. The line went dead.

I tried to redial, but the number was busy. The call wouldn't go through. In the end I just replaced the receiver and walked back to my van.

I was right, I'd touch a nerve! Carlina's response had said it all. She was Patrice. I was sure of that now.

What would she do with this information? I thought. And I wondered at the back of my mind, if news had reached her that I was a wanted man. But for some reason I didn't get that impression.

I decided to stop by Robin's on my way home. And when I got there Robin was about to leave out.

"Ah yu me ah cum look fah!" He said to me. "I wanted to see if you would follow me go'ah Mandeville. I got some furniture to collect from a friend."

Robin wanted me to drive him there, because my van was a little bigger than his. But I was in two minds. Firstly I was tired and secondly I was feeling all mixed up.

I eventually agreed to accompany him, so long as he did the driving and paid for the petrol.

We were going to see his mate Everton, who lived in a ten-bed property up in the hills.

Everton's house was a modern build. It was surrounded by lush greenery. The grounds were well lit, and he had a long driveway and an outdoor pool. When we got there we were immediately offered refreshments, and I could tell by the way he was speaking that he'd spent time living abroad.

Everton was giving Robin some chairs and a few other furniture items, he claimed he no longer had use for. They used to be in his Go-Go club, but the club had recently been closed down. Court-ordered. The place had become notorious for violent outbursts and the last incident was between two men, fighting over a dancer. One of them ended up getting shot. He didn't die, but the incident had breached a previous warning. So the club had to be shut down.

Everton wanted three hundred Jamaican dollars for the furniture. So Robin paid him his money and then we were off.

On our way back I wanted to speak to Robin about my problems, but every time I opened my mouth he would interrupt me.

Robin would not stop blabbering on about how the furniture he'd just bought was a bargain. I gave up trying to talk to him in the end. I sat in the passenger seat, listening to him natter away.

Robin parked the van outside the bar and I helped him unload before going home to Shelly and the kids. When I got in Shelly could see I was feeling agitated.

"What's wrong, Tony?" She asked.

"Nothing!" I replied and went to take a shower. I wasn't sure how I should be feeling. Whether I should be scared or pissed off.

Shelly went to bed early, but I stayed up and watched some TV.

Before long I was dozing off, then the telephone rang. I quickly answered it.

"Who's calling?" I asked.

It was Carlina.

"I booked a flight and will be coming to Jamaica at the end of the week" she said bluntly. "Can you pick me up from the airport please?"

Carlina sounded cold. Not even a hello had she greeted me with.

I listen to her explain that earlier on when I told her I was Mur, she went numb. Even though she suspected it all along. To actually hear it from my mouth, was a bit of a shocker. She said when the phone dropped to the floor, she tried to retrieve it but her fingers wouldn't connect with the receiver.

I took my time to answer, but agreed to collect her before she hung up.

That night I slept on the sofa and woke around three in the morning. I was parched and drank a cold beer.

Carlina wanting to return to Jamaica so soon after leaving wasn't a good sign. What did she know but wasn't saying? I was sick with worry. For when I had asked her why she was coming back so soon, she said she had some unfinished business to tie up.

But what unfinished business could that be? When before she left she said all her business was up to scratch.

CHAPTER TWENTY-ONE

I just about made it to the airport on time. The back left tyre on my van exploded on the way there. Due to a slow puncture. So I had to stop and change the tyre before I could drive any farther.

I was surprised when I saw Carlina. She looked ruffled and worn. Not like her usual tidy self. And she was wearing dark glasses, which I can only assume were there to hide the puffiness of her eyes. You could tell she had been crying.

I hugged and kissed her on the cheek, and as I did so her knees gave way. Instinctively, I grabbed onto her, to prevent her from falling to the ground.

Carlina was weak and she looked stressed.

"Let me push your trolley for you," I offered, and took the trolley from her allowing her to walk freely.

We made our way to the car park, hardly exchanging a word between us, and that mood was present for the entire journey home.

I supposed Carlina was thinking about how she would handle the situation. For over the phone she did mention she wanted to speak with me first, but when she came off the plane, said she had changed her mind and decided it would be best if she spoke when both Shelly and I were present.

Shelly was pleased to see her mother back in Jamaica. However, she was concerned about the urgency?

At the house Carlina freshened up then slept for the rest of the afternoon. She had travelled on an open ticket, so there was no return date scheduled as yet.

She told Shelly she had something important she needed to discuss, and would do this later, when the children were in bed.

Dinner was a quiet event. You could cut the atmosphere with a blunt knife. After we ate Shelly cleaned up whilst Carlina put the kids to bed.

I could hear Carlina talking to them. It wasn't very clear because I was in the front room, so I sneaked and stood by the door to listen. The children's bedroom door was slightly ajar and I watch through the gap as Carlina wiped tears from her eye. She was tucking the children into bed.

"It's all my fault!" She whispered and began to recite a little prayer.

"Put your hands together Sheldon!" She said.
"Gentle Jesus! Meek and mild!
"Look upon a little child
"Pity my simplicity
"Suffer me to come to thee
"Fain I would to thee be bought
"Dearest God forbid it not
"Give me dearest God a place
"In the kingdom of thy grace."

Shelly's stomach had started cramping her again. The twinges were coming back, but getting more severe as the evening went on.

We were all in the front room, and Shelly sat on the sofa beside me. I began to rub her stomach to try and help sooth it, and I could see from the corner of my eye that Carlina was giving us hateful looks. "I hope she wasn't dealing with any jealous crap" I told myself. *That would be foolish.*

Carlina sat upright in the armchair and asked Shelly to switch off the television.

"I have something very important to announce," She said "which may change everyone's life!"

Shelly anxiously got up and turned off the TV.

"I was in my early teens," Carlina started, "And I had been dating Jerry for several months." She looked at Shelly as she spoke. "Jerry had always been a great guy. A really good person, from the very beginning. He was intelligent, good looking, loyal, ambitious. Almost everything any young girl would want in a boyfriend. The only problem with Jerry was he lacked a fun side. He was quiet, and reserved. Plus he was very deep into his education.

I loved Jerry wholeheartedly, but I had a wild streak. My hormones were doing overtime. They were creating havoc in my body, so I was all over the place. Jerry would stay in and study, whereas I would be out with my friends. I liked to rave a lot. Hide and drink, and sometimes mess around with the boys.

Mama knew I liked to go out. She knew I loved to dance, and being a free-spirited person herself, she would never really stop me from doing certain things. I was allowed to go out with my friends, so long as it wasn't no big people company or out raving all-night.

I was disobedient and would occasionally go to the said dances mama never want me to go to. I'd lie dem time deh, and tell her I was staying by a friend in another district.

One particular weekend, I had gone to a dance in Vere, and met this sixteen-year-old guy. I lied to him about my age. Told him I too was sixteen. He introduced himself to me as Mur, and I introduced myself to him as Patrice, which was another lie. Patrice was the name I used when I met strangers.

We had a great night, and the rave led from one thing to another.

I am truly ashamed to admit it now," Carlina cringed, "but Mur and I slept together that same night, and although we had arranged to meet up again, it never happened.

A couple of weeks later I heard that he had gone to England, and to be honest I thought nothing of it and just got on with my life.

Mur wasn't the first boy I had been intimate with, and even though I and Jerry had been together for more than eight months, we hadn't been intimate yet. Jerry wasn't forward like me. So the weeks that followed were my worst. I remember it clear as if it were today. Fretting and

198

praying that my menses would come! I knew I was pregnant, but hoped it wasn't so.

There was no way I could contact this guy. I didn't know where to start. Where he had stayed in Jamaica, who his people were, what his surname was, or even if the name he had given me was real, because I had never heard of the name Mur before.

"It was embarrassing. I had hoped to miscarry, but my baby stayed, and by the time I reached the end of my first trimester, I had to come clean. My waist was clearly expanding. Getting bigger by the week, and I still hadn't told anyone I was pregnant yet. I knew I couldn't keep it hidden from Jerry or my parents for much longer. So I plucked up the courage one day and spoke to Jerry.

"He went mad… Crazy… Jerry was furious as hell! He cussed me out and called me all the nasty names under the sun. It made me feel low. I had betrayed him. He told me he was saving himself to make our engagement or wedding night special, and I had betrayed him. Still regardless of my wrong doing Jerry stuck by me. He offered to take responsibility for the child but made me promise never to reveal to anyone that he wasn't the child's true father. It was foolish of us, to make a decision like that, but we were young, and in our hearts we believed we were doing a good thing.

"Jerry said I wasn't to mention anything about this guy to him anymore, for if I ever disclosed to anyone that he wasn't the father, he would simply abandon me and the child forever.

"A few days later, together we and told my parents about my condition.

Mum was disappointed. She yelled at us proper. Dad on the other hand threw a fit. He tried to rip the flesh off Jerry's bones and had grabbed Jerry by the throat and was thumping him about the house. Jerry had to use all his strength to wrestle with dad, but my daddy was too strong for him. Poor Jerry fought to free himself from daddy's grip and when he did eventually get away, Jerry ran out of the house like a colt.

He never did tell his parents about the attack, and as the months passed, all was forgiven.

I now know hiding the identity of my child's father was the biggest mistake I'd made in my life."

Attentively I listened to Carlina express herself. My bottom lip had dropped within inches from the ground and butterflies summersaulted in my stomach as I waited for her to reveal the identity of this child.

Shelly appeared to be surprised and utterly confused by it all. "Where was that child now, and how old was he or she? *I really wanted to know.*

However I didn't say a word, because I did not want Shelly knowing I was the young boy Carlina was speaking of.

Carlina too looked anxious. "What the hell was she going to say next? It was obvious both Shelly and I were missing something very crucial about this whole situation.

"Was it a girl or boy yu had, Mama?" Shelly asked. "Where is he or she now?"

200

"I'm not done yet!" Carlina said softly.

"What! There's more?" Asked Shelly.

"Anyway, we did what we could to ensure the child was raised well," Carlina continued. "My baby was blessed with loving parents who cherished her deeply, and she grew up to be a very beautiful young woman and a wonderful mother," "But sadly" Carlina whispered "to this day my baby knows nothing of who she really is. My child believes the people who raised her were her biological parents. But she needs to know the truth now, because she is paying a heavy price for the wrong doing of me and Jerry."

Tears welled up in Carlina's eyes. "I just pray my child can find it in her heart to forgive us!" She said. "I hid the truth from her for so long and have caused an abomination. Because the most disturbing situation has now evolved!"

"Weh yu mean, Mama? Weh yu ah try fe seh? Tell me!" Shelly pleaded. "Weh dis ave to do with me and Tony?" Shelly asked, herself as she got ready.

I hadn't even taken into account the age of the child Carlina was talking about, until that very second. Quickly, I jumped off the settee. Shelly was rubbing her stomach and complaining that her contractions were increasing.

"Tony mi need fe gah hospital now! De baby ah cum. Mi feel fe push!"

"Aright get ready!" I said to her. Then asked Carlina to accompany me round the back. I held Carlina by her upper arm and practically pulled her off the chair, before she could decline.

It wasn't sinking in. Shelly hadn't caught on. I knew exactly what Carlina was saying, but I didn't want to believe it. I hastily whizzed Carlina out the back yard. So she wasn't able to respond to Shelly's question just yet. Carlina was trembling like a leaf and could barely move. She knew what she was going to say next was would shatter lives. Nothing would be the same after tonight, and that I believe, was Carlina's greatest worry.

"What are you trying to tell us?" I asked her.

Carlina looked at me hard. It was almost intimidating.

"I knew you were Mur," she hit back. "From the moment I set eyes on you, I knew exactly who you were. It was me you met all those years ago, and it is you who fathered my child!"

"Hush up!" I demanded and put my hand over her mouth to quieten her.

"No!" she said. No more. Carlina was shaking her head and pushing my hand away. "I've kept my mouth hush for too long, and look what it's caused. The child I am talking about is Shelly. Mur you're Shelly's father!" She snapped. Carlina obviously didn't want the neighbours to hear, as she practically whispered those words from her mouth, "And you are also the father of Shelly's children. Don't you realise what this means? Your children are also your grandchildren!"

There was silence. My hands fell down to my sides.

Her words cut through me like a jagged sword and went straight to my heart.

202

"You! You! You!" Carlina cried. She was beating my chest simultaneously. "Shelly is your daughter! *Our* daughter!" She said.

I couldn't listen to anymore and ran into the house to see if Shelly was anywhere nearby. I was so worried she may have overheard her mother. Now was not the time for news like this. Not whilst she was just about to have another baby.

Shelly was still in the front room on the sofa with her bags ready and waiting to be taken to the hospital. She looked uncomfortable and was moaning and rubbing her stomach.

"Shelly are you all right?" I asked.

"I think the baby is coming, Tony!" she said. "We need to go now. To the hospital!"

Before leaving the house, I went back out to see Carlina and warned her not to say another word to Shelly on the matter, or I would kill her. Then I gathered Shelly's bags and put them in the van, and off we went.

Mandeville Public Hospital was about 7.5 kilometres away. It took us just over twenty minutes to get there.

Shelly's water had broken during the drive, and her desire to push was as strong as ever. We got to the hospital parking lot and knew we had just minutes to get her into a labour ward, before the baby would start making its way out.

I rushed to look for a wheelchair, but couldn't see any unused. One of the receptionists explained there had been a fire in Newport, so the hospital was treating more patients than usual that particular night, for smoke inhalation and minor burns.

I literally had to plead with the receptionist to get a chair for us. I let her know my wife was on the verge of giving birth in my van. The receptionist asked a nurse to take a wheelchair from someone who seemed less in need. Then the nurse accompanied me to my vehicle.

Shelly was puffing and panting and trying to stop herself from pushing when I got to the van. She let out a little squirm as the baby's head bared down. I felt so sorry for her, she looked real pained up.

I was thankful she had missed the latter part of her mother's talk. It wasn't the time and surely would have destroyed her.

She had been questioning me constantly, on our way to the hospital. I made up some excuse about Carlina only wanted her to know she had a sibling out there.

The nurse wheeled Shelly into the delivery room and tested her blood pressure before checking to see how far she had dilated.

Shelly was fully dilated and could no longer stop herself from pushing. The maternity team quickly prepared her for delivery and within minutes the baby's head was fully visible.

Shelly gave birth to a healthy seven pound two ounce baby boy that night. It was a quick delivery. Took less than fifteen minutes from our arrival at the hospital until the child was born.

"Look, Tony!" she said, holding the child towards me. "We have another boy. A son. He's lovely!"

I struggled to look at the baby and could only glimpse him briefly. I just couldn't bring myself to look upon the child as I had done with his brother and sister.

It felt like he was an abomination!

Shelly tried to hand the baby to me, but I wouldn't take him. I told her some crap about my clothes being too filthy to hold a new born.

I wanted to leave. Make a quick exit. She was my daughter, and we had been living together as husband and wife for over six years. My heart was in mourning. I had to get out of there.

"I'll be back later!" I said to her as I walked out of the delivery room. I couldn't even kiss her goodbye.

The last time I had shed real tears was when baby Malia passed. But on my way home that night, I cried. I felt sad and disgusted at the same time.

There was no question about it or any point in prolonging what could never be again. I had to terminate my relationship with Shelly immediately. Cease all contact with everyone. I didn't want to face them for now, and began to feel a great sense of anger towards Carlina. Her lies and secrecy had been the cause of this.

It seemed since Phiucha's demise, a chain of events were taking place in my life. Was some unforeseen force be behind it? Trying to push me into committing suicide? Or had Karma come to finish what she started.

Before going back to the house, I stopped by Robin's Rum Bar. I wanted to get smashed (drunk). And I didn't want to see Carlina for now. Not whilst I was still sober. I blamed her for everything.

Shelly and I had brought three children into this world and although we were innocent of our actions, the children were unfortunately the result of incest! *I could not believe the situation presented to me.*

As I approached Robin, he was shutting up shop. "Sell me a flask of rum!" I shouted to him from the van.

"If yu lucky wan more time!" Robin replied. "Mi just ah get ready fe cut out!"

Robin had two bottles of rum in his hand, which he was taking home with him. He handed me one of them and said I could pay him later, or when I'm ready.

I took the bottle and drove over to my place. I was still feeling angry towards Carlina and decided I'd stay in my van for a while, and listen to some music. I put the bottle of rum to my head and took a swig of it.

The drink hit the back of my throat, which burnt, and I shuddered. But once it went down and passed through my chest I felt such a warmth. Soon enough, I was swigging again, and after that I took another one and another until my head was semi spinning.

I began to cuss. Argue with myself. The alcohol was getting the better of me. It was making me irate.

This was the second time I was losing all the significant people in my life. History was repeating itself,

206

despite the fact it wasn't self-inflicted this time round. Carlina was to blame.

"She's not getting away with it!" I kept saying. "No way am I letting Carlina get away with doing this to Shelly and me and the children."

I got out of the van and stormed into the house. I had wound myself up real bad. "Carlina!" I shouted as I shut the door. "COME HERE, NOW!"

The children woke up and began to cry. I had frightened them out of their sleep.

"I'm coming!" Carlina answered sheepishly. She, too, had been sleeping. Carlina walked towards the children's room first.

"Where are you going?" I asked her. "Don't go nowhere near my kids tonight!"

I was hostile and could not stop myself from speaking to her that way. I managed to get the children settled. Then I went into the front room to deal with Carlina.

She was sitting in her usual spot, the armchair.

"How could you?" I asked her. "Why do this to your child?"

I was prancing up and down. "Have you any idea how much grief this is going to cause your daughter, and your grandchildren, and me? My babies are cursed. They shouldn't be here! That's why they are disabled! Their blood, our blood. The line is too close! I am your daughter's father and have been living with her as a husband would his wife. We built a home together, had children together, created a family life. We have been committed to one another for almost six years. This is crazy Carlina! Absolute madness!" I shouted.

"Mi nuh even wan none ah unu inna me yard nuh longer! Not one ah you!"

The more I spoke, the louder and angrier I got. "Yu better tek yuself, yu daughter an fe ar pickney dem outta my ouse before de mont end!"

"What was I saying about my Shelly and the children? I thought. I couldn't believe it! But I couldn't stop myself! It had to be done. I knew Shelly was going to take it hard, but what choice did I really have? There was no way our relationship could continue. Not on my watch. And I wasn't about to tell her that face to face. It was over and that was that. There was no way I could go back.

Besides… What could I say was the problem, if she asks why? What would I tell her? Oh sorry Shelly but I just found out I am your dad? No way!" I argued.

"I loved Shelly, there was no question about that, and I did not want to hurt her. But this pain she was going to feel was inevitable. Our relationship was wrong and illegal and therefore could not continue.

Seeing her again would be complete madness.

"She's at Mandeville Public Hospital," I said to her mother, and then I went to my room.

Carlina had not uttered a word to me. She stayed silent throughout and remained seated in the armchair, crying, as I left the room.

After a few minutes I heard a knock on the door. "Tony! Please try to understand!" She begged.

"Oh go away Carlina!" I shouted from the bedroom. "Leave me alone!"

I had nothing to say to her. I seriously couldn't work this woman out. Why had she waited so long before telling her daughter about her natural father? Yes, she was young at the time. I gathered that. But I just couldn't understand how she could lie to Shelly for so long. Furthermore, I believed she still would not have made any attempt to tell Shelly the truth if this situation had not arisen. I didn't feel now was the right time. Not whilst she was about to have another baby. The damage had already been done. So why not wait until the baby was at least a few months old.

All of Carlina's actions was selfish. Everyone has the right to know who they come from. But there is a time and a place!

"Women like you," I opened up the door and said, "sleep around, and when the baby comes, you think you can slap a man wid the longest jacket in your closet, and keep the true father out of the picture.

A lot ah unu goin meet disgrace! Cah brudda ah go end up wid sister, cousin wid cousin, uncle wid niece, auntie wid nephew and fadda wid daughter!"

Carlina yu's careless." I said. "And not becah yu breed young, but becah yu bring disgrace pon yu pickney. Yu choose fe hide har from har true fadda becah yu shame seh yu gi up you jewels, fe ah one night slam.

I starting to lose my cool and grabbed Carlina by the throat, where I began to squeeze mercilessly.

"What are you doing?" She squealed, and coughed then spluttered. I could see the look of terror upon her face.

"Stop it!" she pleaded. "Please!"

But I could not sympathize. I was closing off her airways and looking in her eyes as the blood rushed to her head. Carlina clenched my wrists and pulled at them. She tried so hard to loosen my grip. But the lack of air was making her weak.

Her eyes bulged from their sockets. She looked at me as if she was going to pass out.

Carlina was losing consciousness and I was losing control. Urine trickled down her legs and onto the floor, and I saw her eyes flicker until they began to slowly close. Only then did I release her.

As soon as I let go, her head flopped and smashed against the passage wall, before she dropped to the ground. Carlina remained completely still for almost half a minute. Then inhaled deeply and chokingly exhaled.

I roughly pulled at her nightgown. "Go and clean yourself up!" I demanded. She cowered, and raised to her feet unsteadily.

*

Carlina then limped to her room to collect her bath stuff then she went into the shower.

She felt her bruises as she washed her skin and kept asking herself how she could rectify the damaged she had caused.

Without a shadow of a doubt Carlina knew Mur was right.

Due to her indiscretion, she and Jerry had concocted this dreadful story and began to live a lie. And even when Jerry had split and left the family, Carlina continued living that lie.

She had hidden the truth from everyone. Even her parent's died believing Jerry was Shelly's father. Why hadn't she let her daughter know that her biological father was a British man living in England! Why had she waited for Shelly to reach adulthood and have children of her own, before she was prepared to spill the beans?

Carlina's lies and secrets had ruined the lives of five people. How in heaven's name was the family going to recover from this?

Her neck was sore and aching, and you could see the shape of Mur's palms and fingers printed right across her throat.

After her shower Carlina went straight to her room and sat at the dresser. She looked deep into her eyes. Then burst into tears, because she knew no matter what she did, there was going to be losers on every side.

*

Carlina woke with a splitting headache. She had spent most of the night crying, and felt nauseous every time she thought of Shelly's situation. Mur had left out from early. She heard him go. And Nicole had come over and taken the kids back home with. She'd left a note.

Carlina felt helpless. She telephoned Terrence to come and pick her up. Then started to pack Shelly and the children's things in cases.

She didn't want anyone knowing what had taken place between her and Mur during the night. Nor did she want anyone to know that she had lied all these years about who Shelly's father was.

As she packed her daughter's belongings, Carlina tried to convince herself she had done the right thing. Mur had certainly given her food for thought.

"Oh, what am I going to do?" Carlina asked herself. Maybe it would be best to tell Shelly she had a sister out there. For now anyway.

There was a knock at the door. It was Nancy, and she was looking for Shelly.

"Shelly's not here!" Carlina shouted from the window.

"Is everything aright, miss?" Nancy asked. "Cah last night I heard shouting and…"

"Everything is fine!" Answered Carlina. She remembered Shelly warning her of Nancy's nosiness.

"Shelly is in hospital. She had the baby last night, and I'm afraid I'm very busy right now Nancy, so you'll have to call back some other time." Carlina wanted Nancy to go.

"Oh, wish Shelly well for me! And tell her I'll pop in to see her when she gets home!" Nancy shouted, then she left.

CHAPTER TWENTY-TWO

My life was in a mess, once again! And I felt the only person I could talk to right about now was Avril. I had left home from early, and driven up north to spend a couple of weeks with her. My plan was to stay there until everyone had moved out.

I knew Avril wouldn't mind. She always had time for me. Said she loved when I was around. Found me intriguing. Unpredictable, unlike her husband who would always give in to her.

"Mi wasn't looking fah yu todeh Tony!" Avril said, when she opened up the door to me.

"I stopped by your workplace first" I explained. "They said it was your day off. So I came here to see you."

"Yu look rough though!" Answered Avril. "Whappen? Trouble at home. Yu never sleep last night?"

"Avril, Avril, Avril!" I sighed hugging her tightly, as I placed my chin upon her head.

Avril was quite short, fairly plump, dark-skinned, and curvaceous. Physically she wasn't really my type, but I found her rather appealing. Avril had long, black, wavy hair, which she wore out and combed back. She had a very pretty face, but what I admired about her most was she was very hard-working, and in recent months I had grown extremely fond of her.

"What's wrong, babes?" She asked. I could tell she didn't want to pry, but was just expressing sincere concerns.

"I got problems!" I sighed. "Big problems! And I cannot even discuss them with you. It's that serious!"

"Hush!" Avril said and kissed me on my bare chest.

We spent most of that morning in bed and in the afternoon travelled along the coast, to inform my customers that I was not going to be delivering any goods to them for the next three weeks.

I was so fed up; for once again I had lost my whole family. There was no question in my mind that Shelly and I were done. Not that I didn't love her or the children. It was simply that whatever was could no longer be. There was no point in prolonging the matter. We had to let go of each other.

I missed everyone, terribly. Nonetheless, the thought of lying next to my daughter as I had been, absolutely revolted me. I figured this was the only way out. Splitting like this. In the end it would be best for both of us.

Shelly wasn't at fault. I knew that. Neither were the children, nor I, but I just couldn't be around them. Face them. I felt so ashamed, even though I hadn't intentionally done any wrong.

I was troubled when I went to bed, but for some reason I slept surprisingly well and woke the next day feeling refreshed and ready for whatever life had to throw at me.

Avril lived in a five-bedroom house on a subdivision of Mango Walk, north east of Montego Bay. Which was an upper-middle-class area that overlooked the Caribbean Sea. She didn't have any worries of prying neighbours sticking their noses in her business, because the area was still in its very early stages of development and therefore underpopulated.

Avril didn't have children, a decision she'd consciously made in her younger years and one she had no intention of altering any time soon. She was a career woman therefore her life was dedicated to her job.

Most of my days at Avril's were spent gardening. I loved working outdoors and with each passing hour had turned her bushy plot into a neat, manageable landscape.

Avril seldom cooked. She would get stuff from the hotel kitchen, so most of our meals were ready cooked. Every now and then I would surprise her with a candlelit dinner. I would make it myself, and we'd sit on the veranda and eat as we looked over at the sea.

We rarely left the house together. Avril's job was very demanding. So she would often return home from work tired and wanting to go bed early.

I enjoyed staying with Avril, but time was drawing near for me to go home. I prayed Shelly and the kids were gone. But needed to make sure of this before I returned to the house.

I had left a note on the dresser. Telling her my mother had taken ill, and I had to take an emergency flight back to the UK. It was all lies. I just thank goodness I'd never ever told her either of my parents' full names, or she probably would have called the 'British Embassy' in search of me. Shelly was under the impression my parents were Mellor's but they were Dera's.

I called Nicole to go and check on the house for me and she called back a couple of hours later to tell me she didn't think anyone had been there for a while. Said she could tell because the curtains had been closed for almost two weeks, and were still closed now.

Nicole was disappointed that I had gone away without notifying her. She asked if she should be seeking employment elsewhere, as she'd not received any wages for the last two weeks. Nicole relied on the weekly money I paid her. It helped to run her home, and school her daughter.

She explained that the day after Shelly had the baby and Carlina came to pick up the children Carlina had asked her to keep an eye on the place. Carlina told her she was taking the children down to Clarendon, until Shelly came out of hospital. But when a week passed and she'd not seen or heard anything from any of them, Nicole called the hospital. The hospital informed her that an Uncle of Shelly's had collected her two days after she had the baby, and that was it. Nicole personally had not seen Shelly since Shelly went into hospital.

CHAPTER TWENTY-THREE

Carlina left the house on the same day Mur went up north. She didn't trust being alone with him anymore. Whilst she was packing her daughter's belongings, she stumbled across their passports so she took them, and told herself if the worst came to the worst, she would buy everyone's ticket, and bring them to America with her.

Terrence came for her after he finished work, and they went to pick up the children before going to the hospital to visit Shelly.

Carlina really didn't know what she was going to tell her daughter, if Shelly asked any questions.

"Where's Tony, Mama?" were the first words from Shelly's mouth, when Carlina entered the ward. Carlina had to think carefully before replying.

She hesitated and remembered the note she'd found on the dresser. "He left you this!" Carlina said as she removed the torn piece of paper from her handbag and handed it to Shelly. The note read.

Hi Shelly,

Sorry but had to leave sudden. Got a call from England. Mum's ill. Booked the earliest flight out. I'm leaving tomorrow evening. Please go to Clarendon with your mother, since I don't know when I'll be back.

Will be in touch,

Tony.

Shelly looked sternly at her mother then asked Uncle Terrence to take the children out of the ward.

"So, Mama!" She turned to Carlina and said. "When im leave?"

"Early this morning," Carlina stuttered.

"A when im get dah call deh?" Shelly asked abruptly.

"I don't know, and can't say!" Answered Carlina.

"Yu sure seh it nuh have nutn to do wid wat you was telling us yestadeh? Cah him was acting kinda strange when mi ask him fe hole de baby. Im never wan look pan de pickney, much less... Is what yu did tell him outta back mama? Member seh me never get fe hear dah part deh!"

Shelly sounded desperate.

"Nuh worry bout it baby girl! Dem tings is minor! When yu come outta hospital we will talk proper!"

Carlina quickly picked up her new grandson and kissed him. "Yu have a name yet?" She asked.

"No. Nuh yet!" Shelly sounded pissed off. "How im can fly out, when me just ave baby?" She tearfully thought aloud.

Shelly was working herself into a state. She was extremely saddened by Mur's sudden departure, and it pained Carlina knowing she was the actual cause.

Carlina felt guilty. Had she not opened her mouth, the situation would not be like this. The only way Carlina could think of helping her daughter, was to take the family back to America with her.

219

She would purchase their tickets and get emergency visas as soon as possible, (which shouldn't be that difficult, considering she had a friend who worked at the US Embassy).

All Shelly needed to do was get the babies details added to her own passport.

Terrence returned to the ward with the children, and when visiting time was over, drove everyone to his house, instead of Clarendon. It wasn't possible for them to stay in Clarendon, because tenants were staying up at their parent's house.

Over the next couple of days, Carlina began to make travel arrangements, and a day later Terrence collected Shelly and the baby from hospital. He took them straight over to Mur's house, which felt empty, dead and lonesome.

Shelly took her time and gathered some things. But that was mainly *children's clothes.* Then she made certain all the electrical appliances besides the fridge was switched off.

Before leaving out, Shelly stood in the hallway, and looked back at the house that she, Mur and the children had shared for the last six years of her life. She was silent and it was at that very moment, something inside told her Mur was gone from her life, forever.

*

Back in England, DSI Phillip Jones had just received news of a sighting in the Caribbean. The detective's informant said they believed that a Mur Dera was living in Jamaica under a different name. But they weren't sure what name that was.

Since the start of the investigation, which was now more than seven years ago, Jones had been given nothing but false leads. Even the information he received about Mur probably being in Mali, had ended up being an absolute waste of time. So Jones wasn't exactly jumping for joy with this recent news of Mur's possible whereabouts.

Nonetheless, Jones had decided from the very beginning he would stop at nothing. After seven years of failure, the idea of success had faded significantly, but it hadn't diminished.

Sightings in Jamaica, meant Jones needed to get on to the Jamaican constabulary, *which he did*, and asked them to be on the alert. But they didn't seem particularly bothered or interested. The Jamaican police had only made one public announcement, that was brief and over a local radio station.

Jones knew whatever leads he had, then he and Sloane needed to go Jamaica, to follow these up themselves. So the officers flew out and hooked up with the Kingston police.

CHAPTER TWENTY-FOUR

I ended up staying with Avril for approximately three weeks, and had spent my last few days touring the beach. I would chat with many of the store owners along the coastline, and before long had begun to notice a white jeep with tinted windows, parked up in every area I went. It would always be nearby, but no driver was ever in the vehicle. I couldn't help feeling there were eyes penetrating me from afar. But assumed it was unlikely; because beside my customers, no one from the north coast knew.

I really enjoyed my stay at Avril's. It helped alleviate a lot of stress. However, the day had now arrived for me to return home. So I hugged Avril by her gate and kissed her goodbye, then I drove off into the sunset. The dirt road was relatively bumpy, and making my car rattle, but there was no way of avoiding it, because it led straight to the main road. As I reached the edge I thought I saw the white jeep again. Parked opposite the dirt road, I was exiting, and it had no driver.

I held my head straight, and turned left. When I was about half a mile down the road I checked my mirrors. I was looking to see if I was being followed. But the jeep was nowhere in plain sight.

I got to my house just before 9pm, and when I turned the key and entered the building, my heart immediately sank. The place looked desolate. And not hearing the sound of my children or Shelly, made it feel kind of eerie. I missed returning to the aroma of cooked food in the house. I couldn't help it! It's what I was used to.

I went straight to the bedroom and sort of hoped Shelly had ignored my letter. But she wasn't there. After a quick look around, I could see that a lot of the baby's things were gone. Shelly's drawers and wardrobe were also practically empty. The same with Antoinette and Sheldon's belongings. Almost all of their clothing was gone.

It was to be expected, but still I couldn't believe I was back at square one. I had all the latest furniture, fixtures and fittings in my house, but no one to share them with.

The place had gathered quite a bit of dust, like Nicole said. So I planned to call her in the morning, to come and clean up.

I wanted a drink, and walked over to Robin's bar and ordered a double white rum and milk.

The bar was packed. A birthday function was taking place. A friend of Robin was celebrating his fiftieth.

There was loud music playing. People were dancing, and drinking and smoking their spliffs. A lot of women were present, and me being Mur, was on them like flies on shit. Flirting and joking around, as per usual.

I began to get drunk fairly quickly, as I hadn't eaten much that day,

After about an hour my behaviour was getting out of control. I was speaking loudly. Doing some foolish dance moves, menacing the women and running my mouth to the men. Some of the punters ridiculed my antics. But others tried to ignore me completely.

I was standing by the roadside, and a white jeep like the one from up north appeared from nowhere. It speeded past this time, and completely freaked me out!

"See me yah!" I started shouting. I was so intoxicated. Come, come get me nuh! Come an get me, unu bastard unu!" I said angrily.

"I hate a coward!" I was cussing, and used two of my fingers to make a gun sign, whilst I waved my hands in the air and beat my chest with my palm.

I felt fearless at that moment. It was the alcohol in my system. The jeep had long gone, but I was still ranting on.

However seeing the jeep had killed my groove. I couldn't stay at Robin's no longer and was indoors before midnight.

Surprisingly, I got up without even a hangover. I had loads of deliveries to do that day, so before I left out I phoned Nicole and asked her to come over and do some cleaning. She had other arrangements, but promised to come the following day.

Things weren't too bad where the deliveries were concerned. My cousin James, had harvest and boxed up much the company's orders for that week. So all I had to do was get them delivered to the customers before any of it had overripe.

All the deliveries I was doing that day were local, but for some reason the more I drove round town, the more uneasy I felt.

One customer in Mandeville had ordered several bags of Irish potatoes, and whilst I was dropping off the order, I saw the white jeep again.

It made me panic and I had to quickly return to my van and make my way back home. I took a couple of weeks to settle into routine again, and for a good while was keeping a low profile. But Shelly and the children would cross my mind practically every day. I wondered how they were doing. For I had not heard from them at all since they left. Although that was my personal choice.

Nicole was still in contact with Shelly. The family were living in America now. Everyone was doing well, and the baby was growing fine. Healthy and strong.

I could only guess what the boy must look like. I hadn't observed him properly when he was born. I'd found it so difficult to look upon the child, knowing what I knew.

I very rarely stayed at home these days. Most of my time was spent with any one of four females that lived in and around my district.

*

A number of months had passed since I and Shelly had separated, and Nicole informed me Shelly kept calling to ask her if she'd seen me at all. Shelly had told her she heard I was still in Jamaica and never did go to England - like I stated in the letter. She wanted to know why I lied to her about my mother taking ill.

Nicole, however, wasn't telling Shelly anything. I had made her one of my girls now, and she was dedicated to me. It didn't matter what Shelly said to her, Nicole wasn't letting Shelly know anything I did not want her to know.

Still employed by me, Nicole would never do anything to risk termination of her employment. Her wages was very competitive. She took care of the house, even though I was hardly there, and was still paid a full wage.

I wondered if Carlina had told Shelly the truth about who I was yet. My life with Shelly was a closed book. I heard her mother was applying for the family's citizenship and I did feel sad about it. But I was relieved at the same time, because it meant I could now move on with my life.

I'd recently got a call from a small citrus company, called Lemora Gralim. They wanted to merge with me. So I was off to meet their representative later that afternoon.

The company had heard I was a supplier of quality foods and felt a merge would be more profitable for both companies.

I needed the extra hands, there was no question of that, and they needed better contracts. So I agreed to meet their spokesperson at an office in Spalding.

When I arrived at the office building I was met by a young lady, who shook my hand and introduced herself as Carmen. She directed me up some stairs which led to a waiting room. The room had several chairs in it, but there wasn't much furniture other than a large full bookcase, a standing lamp in the corner of the room, plus another door which looked like an emergency door.

Carmen offered me a drink and told me to take a seat. She then went back down the stairs, and when she returned, ushered me through the emergency looking door, which was entrance to a small office.

In the office stood a fairly tall man, with his back turned to me. He was straightening a picture on the wall and asked me to take a seat.

"I'll be with you in a moment!" Said the man. Some seconds later, then he spun round and face me. He was young. Very good-looking, but he had a huge scar on his forehead. Instinctively, I thought, *I've seen that face before*, but I could not recollect from where.

"Good day, Mur!" said the man. I was stunned. He had called me by my name. Mur! I looked into his face closely. I definitely knew this man. I'd seen him before, and I recognised his voice.

"Why do you address me by Mur?" I asked.

The young man was very casual about it. Unfazed by my question. "Isn't that your name, Sir?" He said.

I didn't answer. Just kept quiet at first.

"So you think you know who I am?" I queried.

"I do indeed" the man replied. "My mother named me Michael Leon Dera. And I have searched for you for almost seven years now. I was in hospital for two months after the attack. My mother died whilst I was still in a coma. Yes, Mr Mur Simon Dera! I definitely know who you are.

I am your son! The one you almost beat to a pulp and left for dead! I survived your brutal attack."

I gasped when I heard this, and ran to the door in shock. I began to pull at the handle, but the door would not open. Someone had locked it from the outside.

I ran to the window and tried to climb out of it, but when I looked down I saw a police car, plus the notorious white jeep in the car park. There were two uniformed Jamaican officers standing at either sides of the police car.

The driver's door of the jeep swing open and so did the front passenger's door, and out stepped two white men. The right back door of the jeep also swung open, and out stepped a well-dressed black woman. I could just about make her out. It was Carlina.

"That bitch!" I cursed, and watched her point to me and nod, as if she was confirming my identity to the two white men.

Michael again began to speak. "I met Carlina several months back, in a supermarket down in Christiana." He said. "We bumped into one another accidently, and when she saw the mark on my forehead, she asked how I'd gotten such a terrible scar to my face? I told her a man named Mur did it, and he still hadn't been caught yet. I also told her the man had taken my mother's life, and he was wanted by the British police. Carlina took my number and said she might have some news for me. But she couldn't guarantee it.

"Two weeks later, you lost your temper with her, so she contacted me and told me where you lived and what you did. I then got in touch with the British police to let them know I had found you." And you have been under surveillance ever since. Even when you went up to the North Coast to stay.

The office door swung open as Michael was speaking, and Detective Superintendent Jones entered the room. He introduced himself and also introduced Officer Sloane to me. Carlina had accompanied them.

"Is this the man you know as Mur?" DSI Jones asked Carlina, whilst he pointed in my direction.

"Yes! That's him! That's the Mur I know." She said. "Please officer, take him away!" She pleaded.

The superintendent approached me. "Turn and spread your legs!" He ordered and place your hands behind your back"

Then he placed the cuffs on my wrists.

"I have been looking for you for a very long time!" Mr Dera. "And I almost gave up hope. But now I am arresting you under suspicion of the death of Mrs Phiucha Dera, he said and read me my rights.

DSI Jones looked relieved. After all those years of hunting me down, I was finally caught.

The officers led me from the building to the white jeep in handcuffs. The car park was crowded with people by then. I had to hold down my head in shame.

"Say good bye to Jamaica!" Sloane whispered sarcastically in my ear, "Because you, young man, are going to jail for a very long time!"

I didn't even bother looking up. I knew no one would ever believe I had only punched Phiucha once, and not with the intention to cause her any injury. But I had fled the scene. So I looked guilty, and now I was going to prison for murder.

As I sat handcuffed in the back of the jeep, journeying towards the police station, I couldn't help but wonder whether any of this could have been avoided. I now know without a doubt it could have, had we not chose to live a life full of lies and deceit.

ACKNOWLEDGEMENTS

I would like to officially thank all the people who dedicated some of their time to my cause. Those who unselfishly gave a listening ear, when I needed it most and encouraged me to continue, when I felt like chucking it all in.

I love each and every one of you, from the depth of my heart.

Without you guys this book would never have materialised.

So, I want to say to:

Daisy May Carydice *My beautiful mother*, Stefan Carydice *my son*, Jaysharn Carydice *my granddaughter* and Davina Morgan *my adorable niece.* You are my motivators. My main reason for living. Everything I do, is for you. I love you guys more than words can say.

Desmond Spencer, My King. Thank you for your kindness and love, you are my soul mate, the solid rock I stand.

Leanzia Campbell and Josette Dyer, You have seen me go through some of my worst moments and you patiently listened and allowed me to rant on. Even when I was at fault, I could always express myself freely and without reservation in your presence. God bless you ladies.

And to my bonefide from childhood, Angela Darlington. I just love you. Thanks for being you and thanks for your professional head, your honest heart and your loyalty. You are a force to be reckoned with. We date back over four decades and have been through thick and thin, hot and cold, good and bad, happy and sad. Yet still we remain. I wouldn't change that for the world.

I also want to thank my editor Allister Thompson *from Canada* and my book cover creator Sheer genius *from the US*, for making a woman's dream come true.